Sissy Princess

The Story of a Pansy Husband Becoming a Sissy Little Girl by the Hands of His Hot Wife

Vivian Dash

Summary

Preface

1. Ms. Deepika
2. Sanjay
3. Ms. Gemma
4. Clothes
5. Makeup
6. Ms. Deepika's House
7. Ms. Gemma's House
8. Entranced
9. Confessions
10. The Plan
11. Thirsty
12. Late Night Thoughts
13. Rough
14. The Special Day
15. Lay Bare
16. The Condition
17. Princess
18. Not Enough
19. Too Much
20. Someone New
21. Frank "Big Balls" James
22. Princess Meets Frank
23. XOXO
24. All The Things that Mouths Can Do!
25. Love, Sex, Fuck
26. The Pink Room
27. First Time
28. Special Lullaby
29. The Future
30. The Awakening

Afterword
The Author

Preface

This piece was commissioned by a dear client, mixing his guidelines and fetishes with my creativity. It's important to emphasize how sexual fantasies have little to do with a person's real-life and motivations.

As a fetishist that works on different spheres, such as live chats and through the elaboration of custom content (videos and texts), I've encountered all kinds of subjects that could have a controversial aspect if taken out of context.

Sex is still a taboo in the XXI century and many of our intimate fantasies come from a place of shame. Allowing oneself to talk about them, playing them within the realms of imagination in a safe space among consensual adults is a way of catharsis. Releasing these conflictual feelings in a make-believe scenario helps to enable the person's sexual and romantic relationships to be dealt with in a more open and healthy way.

In this book, we talk about some polemical themes, such as BDSM dynamic, feminization, humiliation, cuckolding, physical violence, imposed sexual actions, etc. I can't stress enough that this is a work of fiction with the intention to be played only in the mind.

In real life, all activities must be done through the Safe, Sane and Consensual understanding. It's important to readers to know that behind a kinky scene there must be an agreement between the parties before it takes action, a safe word and the acknowledgment of Personal Responsibility, Informed, Consensual Kink (PRICK) and Risk-Aware Consensual Kink (RACK).

Said that, enjoy the history and if you'd like a debate in-depth about the fetishes explored in this book and how the lenses of sexual fantasy must be free of morals and politics in order to function as a liberation tool, read the Afterword.

With Love,

Chapter 1 - Ms. Deepika

After touring the world being the hottest teacher at the sissy school, Ms. Deepika is back in town. It was right after college that she started turning men into little girls. At the height of 5'11," many of them already had to look up to her as little girls themselves, she found out it came naturally to all these strong handsome men, especially the short ones.

Ms. Deepika has always been a beautiful woman, a hot babe. With her statuesque figure and toned body, long silky brown hair that goes way beyond her small waist. The men can't stop staring anywhere she goes, especially to her beautiful breasts and wide hips, sometimes they even get cross-eyed looking at so much beauty and figuring that they would do anything to be with her. Literally anything, including becoming little girls.

The way she became a teacher at the sissy school was actually a very intriguing story. For a while, she was in love with this other student at college, a very handsome and muscular man called Sanjay. He's smart, successful, and with a bright future ahead. Ms. Deepika always wanted to meet someone like him to share an amazing life together, but there was this one little thing that bothered her.

Sanjay was one of the best students, really good at sports and gym, and with an extremely rare business acumen. But Sanjay was kind of short. At only 5'6", next to Deepika, Sanjay looked like, yes, a little girl. However, that was something Ms. Deepika was willing to overlook because of all his other qualities that far outshined this little thing, but she had to make sure that was the only down side with Sanjay.

Deepika made a plan to seduce the man of her dreams. As they met in college, she would go to class with sexy yet classy outfits that really made all her qualities look fantastic. She would wear high heels making her so tall that nobody would ever look at any other female student. Dresses that were long to cover the good parts but yet tight and revealing enough to show her wonderful body, sculpted daily in the gym.

She loved to play tennis, playing professionally for the university, that's one of the reasons she was admitted in one of the most prestigious centers of high education in the world, perhaps the world. Her excellent grades and fitness prowess made her a special kind of woman. And she wanted someone as good - or even better - than her as her life partner so she wanted to meet Sanjay.

Ms. Deepika was tutoring tennis when she saw her love interest arriving at the tennis field. Her last class was already at the end when he entered the locker room to get hiMs.elf ready. When she saw the beautiful man she knew what she had to do: getting herself available to play with him, hence making herself seem.

Growing up, it was natural for Deepika to seduce men. A born trait, she was so beautiful and interesting she felt that, given the right opportunity, she could have just about any man that she wanted. The woman used her powers wisely, only the top tier of the males would ever enter her radar. Her attention was reserved for handsome, successful, rich, and smart men only. That's why she was so interested in Sanjay, he met all the criteria and she was dying to explore all the good things in life with him.

When Sanjay went to the tennis court, she was there. Looking amazing in her white short tennis skirt, tennis shoes, and a beautiful white top covering just enough of her tall sexy body. It was a sight that nobody could ignore and certainly, Sanjay didn't. He regretted it and she offered a match. He accepted! She was thrilled.

Deepika gave the best of her abilities, she was a professional player after all and it was supposed to be easy to win the game and impress the man. But it turned out it wasn't so easy after all. Sanjay was really good at sports, he knew what to do and when to do it and he actually beat her in her own expertise! Deepika's jar was dropped. Even sweaty he looked so cute, so sexy, and handsome. She had to have him in bed. At the end of the game, she said:

Deepika: Wow you are really good! Congratulations, you won a dinner with me tonight!
Sanjay: So I shall claim my prize, misses..?
Deepika: Deepika - she said, shaking his hand.
Sanjay: Tonight, at Sunset Restaurant, at 8?
Deepika: We have a date!

    She couldn't stop thinking of him the whole afternoon. She got ready for the encounter and even had to touch herself before going, that's how excited she was. It was hard for her to admit that she was in love. But she was! Sanjay was perfect and she would do anything to have him.
    The night came and they met at the restaurant. Ms. Deepika was wearing a beautiful golden dress that covered her toned body perfectly, with a slit to show one of her strong legs. The cleavage was big enough to show the upper part of her amazing breasts. And there he was, Sanjay in a suit, more handsome than he ever looked! A complete gentleman, they had an amazing time chatting and teasing. The way she looked at him, batting her eyelashes and smiling sexily seduced him for what she wanted for later.
    In the end, Sanjay asked to drive her home and Deepika accepted with a plan already in mind. When they arrived, she invited him in. She said she had a surprise for him and they went to her bedroom. Deepika started to undress her sexy dress, teasing him. The way he touched her felt so good, Sanjay couldn't take his hands out of her. They kissed, long french kisses with their hands going all over each other bodies as they were consumed in passion.
    Deepika used her hands to take Sanjay's clothes off. First, his shirt, opening each button and caressing his chest with her

fingers. Then he opened his pants and caressed his legs while taking it all off. When it came to his underwear, Deepika was a bit disappointed. She couldn't see the outline of a hard member waiting for her, she thought he was not that much into her after all... but she pulled it out anyway.

To her surprise, Deepika was faced with a small cock. How could it be real? Sanjay was so perfect in every way. So handsome, with a beautiful smile, his muscular body, and strong arMs.! His witty conversation, his success in every field he ever entered only showed what an intelligent man he was! And there they were, in bed, naked, but his cockette was just... so small!

Deepika decided to ignore that Sanjay had a tiny dicklette and give him a chance. Size doesn't matter, some people say and they were there already, why not try it?

They made love that night, but it was far from what she expected. Sanjay was short in height and he looked like a little girl in bed with her. His cockette was way too small to give Deepika any pleasure, it was impossible to cum with such a microscopic penis. And finally, the sounds he made were not manly at all! He sounded, sometimes like a scared little girl in a horror movie, and sometimes like a chicken, especially when he climaxed.

It was too much to deal with! The love spell broke instantly, she was no longer interested in dating or marrying Sanjay. It was such a shocking experience because she had her expectations so high and he was so pansy, the disappointment was even bigger. Sanjay was the man of her dreams - or any other woman's dream! -, handsome, educated, smart, successful, and such a great kisser. But yet there was this little thing - very little - that totally ruined the experience for Deepika and she was no longer interested in Sanjay and his little girl's sounds. Or any other men whatsoever.

It was the end of the semester and Deepika was able to hide from Sanjay the few times they were in the same location. She graduated in a few months and decided to leave the city for a while, tutoring tennis and maybe find a real man somewhere else.

She sent resumes to many schools in the country and got called by a special board school. They were interested in her services, especially because she was a tall, strong, and sexy woman that could help them make their students the most adorable little girls ever.

When Deepika arrived at the place, she found out that the Sissy School had a special kind of little girls as students. It was a place where married women would enroll their pansy husbands to teach them how to become their own perfect sissy little girls. Deepika loved it and accepted the position right away.

She started only as a tennis teacher but she grew in her Sissy Teacher career. Now her job, as the statuesque tall sexy goddess that she is, involves so much more. Her favorite part is dressing her students at the Sissy School as little girls.

They arrive shy and not really aware of what's going to happen. She loves to take the newbies in and start their preparation, seducing them with her hot body, using her hands to tease them as she undresses them just like once she did with Sanjay in her own bedroom. When they are finally naked, she does something she never did before the Sissy School: she lets them know how small they are!

Ms. Deepika makes sure that the pansy husbands that are her students know how small their tiny cockettes really are, how real men have long and thick dicks with big and heavy manly balls when all they got are girly balls and dicklettes so small that they actually look more like sissy clitties.

She teases them with her hot body, making them want her to touch them more, just so she can use her own hands to dress them up like gay princesses and faggot ballerinas! She finishes them with makeup and wigs with pigtails while they beg for sex. One of the rules in the Sissy School is that little girls must be sex deprived due to their lack of manhood.

Pansy little girls with tiny sissy clitties can never make a woman cum - any woman, be it their hot wives or sexy teachers. So they are teased until they are crying like little girls, having their small cokettes mocked while their girly balls are busted. Ms. Deepika loves her job and the new step in her Sissy Teacher career is to be sent across the world to identify couples that would benefit from the Sissy School and present it to them.

Deepika's first stop was in her hometown and the first name that came to her mind was that handsome man she met once, so strong and muscular, yet so short! So smart and successful yet with a tiny dicklete, a perfect little girl just waiting to be trained. She decided to find out where he was and meet him!

Chapter 2 - Sanjay

As soon as Ms. Deepika arrives in the city, she Googles about Sanjay. It's not a surprise when she finds out he's the CEO of a big company. It wasn't hard to find Sanjay, a rising star in business replicating his personal success in business as well. His Wikipedia page shows an interview where he opens his beautiful house with his wife Gemma, a sexy blonde top model, tall and beautiful. "Poor Girl", Deepika thought, "she looks like a good loyal wife but she's definitely suffering in bed, I can tell".

So she decided that her desire had even more of an important meaning, she would rescue this woman Gemma and help her have the life she deserves, teach her how to turn her husband into a little girl while having a satisfactory sexual life, which must include hunk men with huge cocks, because her husband with his tiny cockette and girly balls could never please her in bed and that's something Ms. Deepika have experienced first hand.

She simply knew that Ms. Gemma could never experience a real mind-blowing orgasm with such a pansy husband. The way he sounds like a little girl when they make love, the way he cries like a scared Indian bride and moans like a chicken when he uses his tiny cockette. Ms. Deepika knew such a gorgeous woman deserved better, than being married to a handsome muscular strong successful man who was something good but his lack of skill in bed could never make her really happy.

It was hard for a loyal good woman like Ms. Gemma to admit it in public, but deep down she knew it. The wife only needed a little hand, someone to show her the way and Ms.

Deepika was ready to show Sanjay's wife the way of happiness, not only for her but also to her husband, Truth is, all these years in the sissy school only showed Ms. Deepika that the ones that most benefit from all these are the sissy husband. Becoming their true selves, becoming little girls for their wives while watching their hot wives being pleasured by real hunk men with big cocks was the biggest pleasure they could achieve.

So Ms. Deepika made the call. Using her contacts she landed Sanjay's personal phone, something that is not listed publicly but a hot well connected woman like herself it wasn't a hard task to get. The phone rang, butterflies in her stomach. Soon a man's voice on the other side answered the phone.

Sanjay: Hello?
Deepika: Hello, Sanjay. Long time no see.
Sanjay: Hey there. Who are you?
Deepika: I'm not sure if you remember me, it's been a long time - she said but she knew he remembered, she was remarkable.
Sanjay: Give me a hint, gorgeous - he said in his naturally charming way.
Deepika: We played tennis together once.
Sanjay: Ms. Deepika!
Deepika: So you remember me after all, darling.
Sanjay: Impossible to forget you!
Deepika: I know. I wonder if you have time to meet me.
Sanjay: I'm sorry but I'm married and... - she interrupts him.
Deepika: A business meeting. I know you are married, honey. Such a beautiful wife you have, Ms. Gemma, am I right?
Sanjay: Yes, and I'm 100% loyal to my hot wife, Ms. Gemma.
Deepika: I didn't intend to make you feel otherwise. I promise you it's 100% business. Can I come over today? What time are you out of work?
Sanjay: Ah, about 6 pm... - he was still unsure about it all but she was so assertive.
Deepika: I'll see you then.
Sanjay: Do you have the address?

Deepika: Yes, I know everything. See you soon, darling.

Ms. Deepika hangs up with a sly smile. She was excited to meet her former lover Sanjay in his successful company. She wanted to take a look at him wearing a suit in all his glory. He was indeed the boss and she wanted to meet the boss on the top floor of the building, in an exclusive place, and remind him that she knew his "little" secret, that he was indeed a little girl.

She spends the whole day getting ready for this very expected encounter. Deepika was so excited to see Sanjay again, he was so charming and handsome and she knew that they would be in each other's life for a long time. He was going to become her new student, her new gay princess!

Deepika wore a nice white female suit, high heels making her even taller than her 6'10" statuesque figure already had. She was tall with long brown locks that would go all the way down her back, making her look so sexy. Her eyelashes were long and curvy making her eyes look so sexy and tantalizing, her lips were full and wet, making her smile irresistible. She made sure everything was perfect to meet the handsome Sanjay again.

When she arrived at the building, she introduced herself at the front desk. All eyes were on her while she walked around with a tight but long white skirt showing her perfect curves and a cute little top under her jacket. She looked like a business but also she was so sexy, everyone in the room could hear her voice saying that she had a meeting with Sanjay, the CEO, and they couldn't not think how lucky he was to meet this sexy goddess.

The secretary said she could go up and she did. All eyes were on her. He was going to meet her on the top floor, a private floor reserved only for the boss for special meetings only. Ms. Deepika was special indeed and the business she had with Sanjay was private and very intimate.

When she arrived, the elevator opened the door and Sanjay was already there waiting for her. The door opened and he could see that sexy goddess walking slowly in his direction. Behind him, the view for the big city, it was right in the sunset, the last rays of sunlight across the few clouds making the sky look blue and pink at the same. It was the perfect analogy of his life, a mix of the blue masculine energy he had to present in his day while covering for his true pink girly energy that hid deep inside because deep down Sanjay was nothing but an adorable little girl.

Like the gentleman that he is, Sanjay stands up and greets Ms. Deepika, and pushes her to a chair next to him. It was a big chair but they were sitting so close to each other, the boss could smell her sweet perfume and couldn't stop looking at her brown locks and bright eyes, as she batted her eyelashes at him in a seductive way. He finally breaks the silence:

Sanjay: What brings you to town, Ms. Deepika?
Deepika: Since I graduated I've left the city for a business opportunity and I'm happy to say that I found my true calling. That's why I'm back and I think you'd benefit immensely from my skills.
Sanjay: Really? Tell me more.
Deepika: My clients are only the best men in the country, darling. The top of the top. Only handsome rich successful men like you - she says in a sweet, seductive but not dominant voice.
Sanjay: And what exactly do you do?
Deepika: You remember the last time we have seen each other. How you cried like a little girl while I was on top of you while we had sex, taking your tiny cokette and that scared chicken sound you made! I know your "little" secret, darling.
Sanjay: aahhh - for a moment he looks down embarrassed of his secret being blatantly spoken out loud.
Deepika: All my clients are like you, honey. I personally use my hands to dress them up like what they really are. Like you really are - she touches his chin and makes him look directly into her sexy eyes - like a little girl.
Deepika: I want to make you my sweet gay princess - she says as she touches his legs in a sexy seductive - I make my clients big strong rich men into little girls and sweet gay princesses! I dress them up with my own hands and force them to be gay. They kiss their hot wives but also strong tall hunk men with huge cocks and

they are so happy about it.
Sanjay: I... Listen, Ms. Deepika - he looks at her wristwatch - I have guests waiting for me at home and I really have to go, I'm so sorry for cutting it short, I have to go - Sanjay says as he proceeds to leave in a hurry.
Deepika: That's ok, darling. I'll finish what I started. You are my pansy princess, my one and only, my favorite little girl and there's no escape!

Sanjay leaves the building with his heart beating so fast and a strange feeling, he is scared like a little girl. He has felt it before that day when they met after the tennis match. He knew how strong and powerful and dominant she was. Of course, he remembers how much he cried like a little girl when they made love. When that gorgeous tall perfect goddess was on top of him and he felt like a little girl under her.

He tried to erase that scene out of his mind and the only woman he ever had after Ms. Deepika was Ms. Gemma, his wife, and they only had sex after marrying. He was afraid that Ms. Gemma, another tall and perfect goddess that he loved so much would run away from him just like Ms. Deepika that never called and purposely hidden from him in the last months before graduating the university,

But for years he felt safe, married to a loyal sexy, and perfect woman like Ms. Gemma, who would overlook his "little" problem as long as he trained really hard at the gym and was a successful rich businessman, gave her everything she deserved. Late at night, sometimes he sat down while she slept, thinking about how he was actually a scared little girl and gay princess hidden in a strong successful man's body.

Now it seems it was inevitable, his fate came back to him and all he could do was try to run away from the one and only other person who knew he was indeed a little girl in denial.

Chapter 3 - Ms. Gemma

The next day, Ms. Deepika enrolls in the best gym in town. Her statuesque figure and beautifully toned body need to be exercised with the most proficient teachers and newest equipment. She wears hot tight black leggings with sheer straps on the sides and a black sports bra to hold her magnificent breasts. Deepika loves to dress to impress.

As soon as she arrives at the gym, to her surprise she soon sees a familiar face: a very tall blonde woman, wearing a tight purple gym jumpsuit. Her pretty blonde hair, so bright and well done, was stunning. Nice looking eyes with sexy eyelashes could mesmerize anyone who looked at her. Cute full lips and a lovely smile. This woman was remarkable and it was impossible to not recognize her from the Wikipedia article, it was Ms. Gemma, Sanjay's hot wife right there!

Too good to be true, Deepika perceived it as a sign that she was on the right path. She couldn't miss the opportunity to befriend this gorgeous woman and put her plans with Sanjay in motion. After all, it was Deepika's true calling to make handsome, smart, rich, and successful men become little girls. And she was going to make sure Sanjay would become the most adorable little girl ever for this wonderful sexy vixen, Ms. Gemma.

During the workouts, Ms. Gemma and Ms. Deepika exchanged looks here and there, there was a spark between the two hot babes. At some point, Deepika finally decided to introduce herself to Ms. Gemma.

Deepika: Hello there. Your outfit is so nice! Do you mind me asking where did you get it?
Gemma: Oh hi! Not at all, I've them custom-made at a store because I'm very tall and not all shops have my size.
Deepika: Oh my god, I totally understand your struggle. I'm 5ft 11 and suitable clothes are so hard to find!
Gemma: I've just finished my workout and I'm going to go there right now, if you want to come with me, it will be my pleasure to show you the place.
Deepika: For sure! What a coincidence I've just finished as well. Let's go!

    The two tall babes head to the locker room. Deepika observes Gemma slowly undressing, first the straps fall down on her shoulders and she pulls them down, revealing her perfectly shaped big boobs. Her white skin, plump breasts, and pink areolas are so sexy and alluring, Deepika can't take her eyes off of Gemma.
    The hotwife kept taking her clothes off. Now it's mid-waist, she pulls harder and it goes below her bottoMs., her beautifully wide hips swaying provocatively as she finally yanks the whole bodysuit down her long strong legs. Gemma knows she's being watched and deep down she likes it.
    Deepika observes the other beautiful woman wondering about all the sexual energy repressed because of lack of orgasMs. from her husband Sanjay and his tiny cockette. She undressed herself while scrutinizing Gemma's body with her hungry eyes. When the two hot babes were completely naked, she touched Gemma's back, who jumped in surprise, then smiled.

Deepika: Oh sorry, I didn't mean to scare you...
Gemma: No, it's ok. It's just that your hands are so soft, your touch...
Deepika: I'm known for my tender touches, on my job - she says as she runs her strong hands all the way down Gemma's back, causing a chill down her spine.

Gemma: Really? Your hands feel so good when you touch me like this. What kind of job did you say you have?
Deepika: I'm a teacher... a special kind of teacher. I help married women like you to find pleasure that has been denied for a very long time.
Gemma: How do you know I'm married?
Deepika: Besides the big ring? I recognize you from the magazines, actually, I studied with Sanjay at the university and I gotta confess we had a brief fling.
Gemma: Wow that's... Such a coincidence - she says as her cheeks get red.
Deepika: How's your married life, Gemma? - her two firm sexy hands grab Gemma's waist and pull her to her naked body, making Deepika's tits rub against the other woman's back.
Gemma: I love my husband, more than anything.
Deepika: Sanjay is a very handsome man, so strong and sexy, successful in all aspects of life - she says as she rubs her pelvis against Gemma's butt.
Gemma: We have a great sex life.
Deepika: You do? Because I know about Sanjay's little problem. Very small indeed, like a little girl - her thick long finger now is caressing Gemma's inner thighs.
Gemma: We love each other - her voice fades into a moan.
Deepika: I remember him in bed, in our mid-twenties in college. I don't think anything down there can grow past that age so I'm pretty sure his dicklete is still small. I remember how he sounded like a little girl when we made love...Isn't it small - Deepika's fingers touch Gemma's perfect pussy, putting her in ecstasy.
Gemma: Yes, I love my husband but he has a small cockette and girly balls.
Deepika: My job is to help women like you find real pleasure with sexy tall studs with huge cocks!
Gemma: No! - she says as she pulls away from Deepika's touch, clearly offended - I'd never do that to my husband, I love Sanjay more than anything and I'm loyal to him.
Deepika: I know you love him, Sanjay is such an amazing man, and

that's why both of you will benefit so greatly from making him become the most adorable little girl - she whispers softly inside Gemma's ears as she brings her close again.

Deepika: In my line of work, wives bring their husbands to me at the special Sissy School. I want to teach you how to use your hands to dress him up and make your husband your pansy princess. Teasing a once strong, successful man like Sanjay into tears, crying like a little girl, will make your marriage so much stronger!

Gemma: I don't want to hurt Sanjay, I love my husband - she can barely contain her moans as the other hot babe touches her intimate parts with her sexy fingers in ways she was never touched before.

Deepika: It will be so hot when I teach you to condition your husband through seduction and denial. That's what I do to make these strong men become little girls. They talk like little girls, walk like little girls, and better yet dress like a little girl pansy gay princess.

Gemma: I'll never do such a thing with my beloved husband Sanjay, but what exactly do you do to them?

Deepika: I grab their girly balls with my hands - she says as she grabs one of Gemma's amazing boobs with one of her hands - and massage them, making them so desperate to be touched in their cockettes. They beg and even cry like little girls until I finally touch their tiny dickletes.

Gemma: And then?

Deepika: Then I use my sexy fingers to jerk off their tiny cockettes in a hot handjob, calling them my little girls. When they are very close to climax I take my strong hands away and teach my sissies how to beg like the little girls that they are - she says using her sexy fingers to rub Gemma's horny clit.

Gemma: Do they all have tiny dicklettes?

Deepika: All my little girls have sissy clittles and pansy balls, that's why the wives inevitably find hot studs with huge cocks. I love to jerk my little girl's dicklettes and remind them what a sweet gay princess they are. They beg and cry like little girls, can you believe that at the peak of excitement they try to grab my body?

Gemma: And what do you do to them?

Deepika: I use my sexy hands to beat them up lovingly with slaps. It's always intended to teach them and I say "good, little girl" when they act right. I also twist their ears until they stop and remind them "that's a sweet gay princess" - her fingers are soaked wet in Gemma's juices as she drives the other woman close to climax.

Gemma: And what happens when they don't stop?

Deepika: I also squeeze and twist their pansy balls making them cry like little girls, but always with a smile on their faces as I tell them "how should a pansy cry, little girl". Tiny cockettes can't make women cum so they are not allowed to cum either, no sex for my sweet gay princesses!

Gemma: This is so evil! I could never allow my husband to be treated like that, I love him too much.

Deepika: But you recognize that his dicklette could never make you cum or remotely feel like what I'm making you feel with just my fingers, because even my fingers are bigger than his sissy clitty - she says as she goes faster fingering Gemma's perfect pussy.

Gemma: Yes, my husband Sanjay and his small cockette could never make me cum, but he is perfect on everything else. Ahhhh - she moans.

Deepika: I teach my little girls how to rub their sissy clitties using only two fingers - she puts two fingers inside Gemma's pussy now - I teach them how to masturbate like a little girl. Just like this - she finishes her most erotic finger movement bringing Gemma to climax.

Gemma: Ahhhh it feels so good - she groans sexily as she cums on Deepika's thick strong long fingers.

Deepika: And my little girls love to watch their hot wives cumming to big cocks, when they find new hot stud boyfriends and make love to them in front of their sissy pansy of husbands.

Gemma: That's very interesting Deepika, but seriously I don't think this is for me. I have a very happy marriage, let's just go to the fitness shop, shall we? - she recomposes, coming back to reality with a post orgasm clarity.

Deepika: Yes, dear. Let's take a shower and go!

Chapter 4 - Clothes

After meeting at the gym, the two hot babes drive to the shopping mall. They head to a special store that makes high-quality products for tall sexy ladies like them. Ms. Deepika loves the garments and starts to select skimpy clothes for herself.

Gemma: Wow, Deepika, these are very sexy outfits! Are they for you when you teach your classes at the Sissy School?
Deepika: Yes, Gemma. I use special sensual skimpy clothes to tease my little girls, they get so turned on by my lustful body, it's easier to control my sissies like this.
Gemma: Can they control themselves when they are next to you?
Deepika: It's very hard because my little girls get so naughty! They try to grope my sexy body with their little girl's hands so I have to constantly slap them away with my own strong hands!
Gemma: I bet you love the attention though.
Deepika: I won't lie, Gemma. It's very flattering to realize the power it takes to make all these strong handsome successful men turn into little girls. Men just like your husband Sanjay.
Geema: I told you I don't want to talk about it, Deepika.
Deepika: I'm sorry, it's just... Sanjay is just a perfect candidate to become a little girl. He is so good looking, his face is beautiful, his body is strong and muscled, he is a hottie, Gemma!
Gemma: I know, I love my husband so much!
Deepika: And besides having such an amazing body, he is very intelligent. No wonder he is so rich and such a famous and pros-

perous businessman. It's not just luck, he is very smart and witty, so fun to talk to.
Gemma: Sanjay is the best company in the world, I could not trade him for any other men like you suggest.
Deepika: You'd not trade him, darling. He'll still be your husband and you'll still love each other, a hot stud would only add to your relationship, not subtract.
Gemma: Enough of this! - she firmly says, offended by the suggestion of cheating on her beloved husband.

The two beautiful statuesque women keep shopping for clothes and Deepika helps Gemma to choose some very nice outfits and lingerie, beautiful, sexy, classy, and skimpy at the same time. She promises Gemma that it will enhance her sexual life.

Gemma: Are you sure these are going to look good on me?
Deepika: I'm one hundred percent certain, my dear. You will look like a goddess to your husband and he will be even crazier about you!
Gemma: How do you know so much about clothes, Deepika?
Deepika: You said you don't want to hear about it, but now you are asking - she giggles - Well, I'm only telling you this because you are curious.
Gemma: I'm sure these are harmless questions, I'm just intrigued by your amazing fashion sense.
Deepika: Of course. Well, at the Sissy School I'm also responsible for dressing the once strong successful men into becoming little girls. The dress-up is a very important phase and I use my own bare hands to make sure they are wearing the cutest gay garments, like good little girls.
Gemma: You make it sound fun!
Deepika: Because it IS fun! First I strip them out of any male clothes they are wearing, using my perfectly manicured hands to touch them for the first time. Usually, these first touches and contact with my strong hands are enough to turn them on.
Gemma: Do they misbehave?

Deepika: As I'm wearing sexy dresses with big cleavages, my little girls always try to grab my big beautiful boobs. I have to beat their hands away as I giggle, smiling sexily and batting my eyelids at them. My sissy gay princess gets hypnotized by me!
Gemma: You are such a goddess!
Deepika: Then after I have a little girl naked in front of me, it's time to doll her up as an innocent, helpless little girl. A real pansy sweet gay princess! The first piece of clothing I got was panties.
Gemma: What kind of panties?
Deepika: Little girl's panties, of course! A sissy faggot must wear pink frilly cute panties to cover her little ass, sissy clitty, and girly balls!
Gemma: That sounds cute!
Deepika: I use my hands to put the panties over my little girl's legs. First I make her get one foot up and inside the hole, and then the other until she has panties on her ankles like a sweet gay princess!
Gemma: Why pink panties?
Deepika: It's my little girl's favorite color! My hands are all over my little girl's leg, pulling the panties up and adjusting the band at every inch. I want to make my sissy faggot pansy feel the smooth fabric rubbing against her skin as I dress her up. And I always compliment "You are looking so good, like a little girl".
Gemma: You are so loving to them!
Deepika: Of course, I want all the best for my little girls. I also grab the sissy clitty as I finish dressing my little girl up and massage it, jerking it off with two sexy long fingers.
Gemma: That's naughty!
Deepika: It's definitely one of my favorite parts. When my little faggot gay princess gets too touchy with me, trying to grab my tits or butt, I slap her little girl's hands away and then squeeze and twist her girly balls.
Gemma: Do they cry, Deepika?
Deepika: Yes, like scared little girls in horror movies! They cry and beg like pansy gay princesses, it's cute and makes me giggle. I love to look at my little girl only with panties on, her sissy clitty so hard inside the pink pair of panties. It's like the cockette is locked inside

because little girls with sissy clitties can't make women cum, so they have no use for their dicklettes anymore!

Gemma: You are evil! - she says playfully and giggles.

Deepika: It's my job, as a teacher of the Sissy School, to teach the once handsome successful men to become little girls. to dress them up like sweet gay princesses! It's truly a source of the ultimate joy for me when I give them back to their wives, wholly trained like the most adorable little girls.

Gemma: What other clothes do you use on them?

Deepika: After putting the panties on, I use my hands to clasp the bra on their back. I always get a matching set of pink bras and panties. You see, little girl panties are easy for them to accept because they are used to covering that area with underwear. But when I finally get a bra for my little girls to use, this is where many draw the line and start to struggle.

Gemma: Do they fight you off?

Deepika: Some of my faggot sissies will try to argue! They start saying no and soon are crying like little girls. I don't give in, my firm hands go to their chest and adjust the pink bra, making them look like gay princesses to me!

Gemma: I bet they look cute with a nice bra and panties set!

Deepika: After the cute pink lingerie set is on, it's time for the outfit. Each husband brought to me gives me a different vibe and I like to match their personality to the first outfit they will ever wear in their new life as a little girl. Sometimes they will be a ballerina, sometimes cheerleader, others go with a maid outfit. I save the princess dress only for my most special sissies!

Gemma: I wonder which one you'd choose for Sanjay.

Deepika: Are you really picturing Sanjay in a sweet gay princess dress? You and I know he would become a little girl princess because he is the most elite alpha level of man there is, therefore he would become the most adorable cute little gay princess ever!

Gemma: No! I'm not imagining that, I love my husband way too much. It was just a silly thought and it's gone now.

Deepika: When I dress up my little girl with a dress, I use one of my hands to put the dress over her head and the other to rub her sissy clitty inside her pink panties. For a moment, she's blindfolded by the pink tutu dress and the lack of sight only enhances the feeling down there, my strong sexy fingers rubbing her cockette until she moans making pansy noises like a little girl.

Deepika: Knowing that my little girl is aroused already, I put my hands on the dress and pull it down to cover her little girl's body. Using my strong hands to adjust every inch of the dress, first over her little girl's shoulders, then on her back and belly, ultimately on her pansy waist, finishing the dress up making her look like a sweet gay princess!

Gemma: I bet they look very cute, you have really good taste for clothes.

Deepika: Thank you. But do you know the most intriguing part of all these?

Gemma: What?

Deepika: Even if you allow me to make Sanjay a little girl for you, I couldn't buy his little girl outfits here.

Gemma: I'm not allowing you to make my beloved husband Sanjay become a little girl. But I'm curious, why would you not buy it here?

Deepika: Sanjay is handsome, strong, muscled, and smart. He is a rich successful businessman and he leads his company as a great leader. He is almost perfect, of course only you and I know his little girl, the fact that he has a tiny cockette and girly balls. But there's also another thing about Sanjay...

Gemma: What?

Deepika: He is so short! And this is a store for tall women only! His sweet gay princess dress would have to come from a little girl store, he has the perfect size of a little girl!

Gemma: Enough, Deepika! This is not funny - she says, being protective of her husband.

Chapter 5 - Makeup

The two hot babes finish buying clothes and take a walk in the mall carrying their bags. They are both tall and slender, with long sexy toned legs in high heels. Ms. Gemma has blonde locks that end right below her shoulders, her eyes are mesmerizing with long eyelashes, full perfectly outlined lips that frame the most warming smile. She has a set of perfect rippled big natural tits, a tiny waist, and wide hips, what the old grandmas call a "breeder hip" like she's ready to be a mother.

The blue dress that Ms. Gemma is wearing wraps her perfect 5 feet 10 inches curvy body in a very sexy way. Ms. Deepika, on the other hand, is wearing an orange dress, a bit shorter than Ms. Gemma's. She has long light brown hair that goes all the way down to her back, beautiful big sparkling brown eyes, and a big smile. Her boobs are a bit smaller than Ms. Gemma's, but also beautiful and perky.

As they walk on the corridors, every man breaks their necks to catch just a little more of the amazing sight that is these two goddesses walking together. They stop to look at showcases and decide to enter a makeup store.

Ms. Gemma grabs lipstick and a new eye shadow palette. Ms. Deepika chooses a dozen lipstick, face creams, blushes, and several eye shadow palettes.

Gemma: I didn't mean to police your shopping, but you just bought yourself quite a collection!
Deepika: Oh dear, I wish it was all for me! I need these for my little

girls.

Gemma: You are kidding me! Do you really make these men... I mean, these little girls - she says uneasily - wear makeup?

Deepika: Of course! My little girls look so cute with the right makeup on!

Gemma: I notice you didn't buy any brushes to apply the makeup tho.

Deepika: Here's a thing about training pansy sissies to become the most adorable little girls: you have to always show them you are in charge, and for that, you have to use your own bare hands. To dress them up, to put on makeup, and to play with their sissy clitties.

Gemma: So after you use your own sexy strong hands to dress your little girl in panties and bra, and then put on a sweet gay princess dress, you also do makeup?

Deepika: Yes, being a heartbreaker goddess is not so easy, it requires many skills. One of them is how to apply makeup to your little girl. Take note that it needs to be waterproof makeup, otherwise it ruins when they cry.

Gemma: I'm not taking notes, I'll never do it to my husband, I love Sanjay way too much.

Deepika: You imply like I'm doing a bad thing to my pansy sissies, but my little girls receive the best treatment in the other and this changes their life and their wives' lives for the better.

Gemma: Why don't you give me some makeup tips? It's not for Sanjay, mind you, I just want to learn more about makeup for myself.

Deepika: Of course, dear. After dressing my little girl like a sweet gay princess with the cutest princess dress, I grab a strong foundation like this one - she puts some on her finger and start to apply to Gemma's face - I use my thick fingers to rub it all over my little girl's face, giving special attention to the forehead. Also never forget the neck.

Gemma: Your finger is so firm - she says, enjoying the gentle yet strong touch of the other woman on her face.

Deepika: After I apply the foundation with my fingers, it's time to

get blush all over my little girl's cheeks, right here - she says rubbing her fingers on Gemma's cheeks - But you are not a little girl, Gemma, you are a stunning hot woman so I'm not going to put blush on your face, you don't need it.
Deepika: Now the lipstick. Please pout. Well done. I rub the lipstick at the tip of my fingers and smear it first on the lower lips and subsequently on the upper lips.
Gemma: What about the eyes?
Deepika: I love to use nude and pink pallets over the eyes to make my little girls look very girly. I rub it with my fingers and then gently massage my little girl's eyelids like that.
Gemma: Wow this makeup is fantastic! I'm feeling so beautiful right now.
Deepika: You are a very beautiful woman, Gemma! I love makeup and being able to do it to my little girls is very fun. I use a lot of makeup on them to cover any reminiscence from their past male life and turn them to into perfect pansy faggot ballerinas!
Gemma: I bet the touch of your fingers and hand over your little girl's faces make them crazy for you.
Deepika: To be honest, many of them don't like it at first. I learned how to put makeup on a little girl with one hand while I'm working with the other hand under her dress, rubbing her sissy clitty and making her cooperate with me.
Gemma: What if even after rubbing their tiny cockettes they don't want makeup?
Deepika: Then I have to squeeze her girly balls and make her cry out loud like a little girl!
Gemma: So after the makeup, are they completely done?
Deepika: Not yet! I also use wigs on the faggot sissies. I chose a beautiful wig for my little girl, something that matches the shape of her face and her outfit, to make her an adorable little girl!
Gemma: Wigs are interesting!
Deepika: Gay sissies get so pretty with a wig on! After I adjust the wig with my hands, I also comb the hair with my long fingers and then make pigtails on each site.
Gemma: A real little girl!

Deepika: Little girls at its finest! I love to tell them how much of a little girl they look at each segment. Then when I'm finally done, I grab my phone and take pictures.
Gemma: That's intense!
Deepika: I know! I bring a mirror and tell my little girl to look how pretty she is. I make her give a twirl and make her sweet gay princess dress swing. Then I make her move the head to the side so her pigtails move, the blush and giggle like gay, little girls. And I take pictures to send to their wives back home.
Gemma: And do they like the pictures?
Deepika: Of course! The first time a wife sees her little girl sissy of a husband dressed like an innocent, helpless little girl pansy in a cute sweet gay princess dress and sissy faggot makeup is remarkable. They never forget this exciting moment!
Gemma: Do they stay still for the pictures?
Deepika: The training is very important so they learn how to sit pretty like good little girls. In the beginning, they don't want to take pictures so I have to lovingly slap their faces. I tell my little girl that she needs to behave and use my strong hand to slap across her face very hard until she behaves. Then I say "What a good little girl you are" when she finally behaves.
Gemma: You also told me you do something to their ears...
Deepika: There are occasions that only slaps are not enough. Or because a little girl gets too flustered and tries to grope my boobs or booty, or because she struggles and doesn't want to let me dress her up or put on makeup. When a slap is not enough, I hold her ears between two fingers and twist them. Sometimes I pull my little girl's ear to make her walk or move her head in the right direction. There are also the girly balls.
Gemma: Even inside the panties?
Deepika: Oh dear, there's no problem to pull the panties down a little bit. I use my hands to tug it just enough so my little girl's sissy clitty and pansy balls are showing. Then I put her girly balls inside my hands and squeeze them really hard until she cries like a scared little girl. I love when she sounds like a virgin Indian bride on her nuptial night.

Gemma: I understand now why you only use waterproof makeup!
Deepika: I want my little girls to look very pretty all of the time, including when they have a river of tears falling down their cute eyes.
Gemma: Thank you so much for doing my makeup, Deepika. This came in handy as today is a special day for Sanjay and me and he is taking me out to dinner.
Deepika: That's wonderful! Is today your marriage anniversary?
Gemma: Actually it's the date that we had our first kiss. He is very romantic and always remembers every milestone in our relationship and makes sure to treat me like a queen.
Deepika: Sanjay seems to be a wonderful husband!
Gemma: He is the best there is. I love my husband so much, he already sent me flowers this morning before I left for the gym. And I bought a special lingerie for tonight.
Deepika: You'll have to tell me all about your special night some other day!
Gemma: I would love to see you again to chat!
Deepika: What about you come to my house tomorrow for tea if you are free during the day. What about 3 pm?
Gemma: Yes, certainly. Text me your address and I'll be there.
Deepika: That's perfect. I wish you an amazing love night with your beloved Sanjay. And I see you tomorrow.
Gemma: See you! Bye.

    The two babes parted in different ways. When Ms. Gemma went home, she knew Sanjay would be home earlier because they were going to celebrate their first kiss by having a fine meal at a great restaurant and drinking some wine, which would lead them to make love in their master bedroom.

    Deepika had many plans in motion, she wanted her to encounter with Ms. Gemma the next day to be perfect and make her open up about the inevitable disappointment with Sanjay's little cockette. After talking about it so many times during the day, it will be impossible for Ms. Gemma to forget that it indeed looks like a sissy clitty and that Sanjay's balls are so girly.

It was all part of Ms. Deepika's plan to turn Ms. Gemma into a heartbreaker hotwife and turn Sanjay into the most adorable little girl in the world. This couple has so much potential.

Chapter 6 - Ms. Deepika's House

The next day comes and at 3 o'clock the bell rings. It's Ms. Gemma arriving at Ms. Deepika's new house. Ms. Deepika walks to the door, she's wearing tight leggings covering her long sexy legs and a tight shirt, it's a comfortable yet sexy combination showing her well shapely figure.

When opening the door, she comes across the beautiful Ms. Gemma. There are very few women in the world as beautiful as this blonde bombshell and it's always fascinating to lay eyes on her. Ms. Gemma is wearing high heels and skinny jeans with a buttoned shirt that lends an air of casual elegance. The last button is open because her boobs are too big to stay completely confined into the shirt, with every step she takes her boobs bounce showing a little more skin out of her clothes. Ms. Gemma is carrying a little box.

Deepika: Hello, dear! Welcome to my new home! Please don't mind me, I'm still unboxing!
Gemma: It's ok, I know how hectic it gets after moving to a new house and what a lovely home you have here in the city. I brought you a housewarming gift.
Deepika: Thank you so much! - She opens the box and finds a waterproof foundation cream from a fancy foreign brand - Oh my God, Gemma! This is THE best foundation in the world and so hard to find in this country.
Gemma: I know, I brought from one of my trips abroad with Sanjay and thought you'd like to try with one of your… little girls -

she giggles as she says the last words.

Deepika: I certainly will! Interestingly, you thought about bringing something that I can use professionally, I guess you have been thinking about the stories I told you yesterday.

Gemma: Oh not in the way you are thinking, you naughty lady. I'm not thinking about submitting Sanjay to your little girl's sissy training. But I confess your stories are quite fun to listen to, such a different life you live!

Deepika: It is indeed very remarkable, I have a true passion for turning strong successful men into little girls. But enough of me, I want to hear all about your romantic night!

Gemma: There isn't much to tell - she says as they sit down on the sofa - We went to that new seafood restaurant up the avenue, we have been wanting to try it. It's such a beautiful place, we had a lovely evening and then you know, adult stuff in the bedroom - she blushes and giggles.

Deepika: Are you really going to leave me thirsty for the details?

Gemma: I'm not as eloquent as you are, dear. At least not in this department. I prefer to hear your stories, I believe they are quite more interesting!

Deepika: As you wish! - Ms. Deepika pours a glass of wine to each of them as they keep talking.

Gemma: You always refer to your little girls are sweet gay princesses. Does it mean that... You make them become gay?

Deepika: It's part of the training to make my little girls accept their wive's hot stud boyfriends with big dicks. I told you before that this dynamic benefits both parties, husband and wife.

Gemma: How so?

Deepika: As soon as I finish dressing my little girl in her sweet gay princess dress, I tease her by talking about hot boys. I put one of my sexy fingers over her lips and told her how good she would look with a big cock in her mouth. They always tremble like a sissy gay little girl!

Gemma: So devious!

Deepika: Can you imagine using your sexy and perfect manicure hands to hold Sanjay's strong manly hands and force him to feel up to big, strong men with big sexy cocks? Sanjay would go crazy and accept you to have a hot stud with a massive cock and big balls as a boyfriend in a heartbeat!

Gemma: Stop that, Deepika! I don't want a stud for a boyfriend, I'm pretty content with my husband and I'm loyal to him. You are offending my honor by talking about these things.

Deepika: I'm sorry dear, it's just that this image can't get away from my head.

Gemma: Just stop it! Think about your little girls sissies.

Deepika: Alright. Do you know something that I love to do to them? - she says excitedly.

Gemma: What?

Deepika: I love to grab my little girl's sissy clitty on my hand and rub it while I teach her how to say gay girly statements!

Gemma: What kind of gay statements?

Deepika: For example, I jerk off my little girl's sissy clitty with two of my sexy fingers and tell her "Now say that you love boys". And my little girl will say with a soft girly voice "I love boys". It's so cute! Then I tell my little girl "be a good girl and tell mommy how much you love being Ms. Deepika's little girl and pansy".

Geema: And do they say this?

Deepika: When a little girl struggles and doesn't want to say, I grab her pansy balls and squeeze them on my hands, ballbusting her. Very quickly she says, with tears running down her face in a little girl voice "I love being Ms. Deepika's little girl and pansy".

Gemma: You are so creative!

Deepika: It's part of the training for my sissy faggot princess to do little girl's affirmation to be convinced that she is nothing but a little girl pansy of a husband. I especially love when I tell my little girl "now tell me you are my sweet gay princess". And my little girl will say "Ms. Deepika, I'm your adorable sweet gay princess eeee" while she cries because I'm twisting her pansy balls.

Gemma: I feel bad when you say you make a little girl cry.

Deepika: Oh don't feel bad. It's part of being a little girl to cry like a little girl. And sometimes a little girl will also make weird sounds like a chicken or a duck while crying, it releases endorphins and makes little girl's more open to my suggestions. Besides being cute and funny, it makes me giggle.

Gemma: Do all these strong successful men really sound like little girls? How is it possible?

Deepika: It's all part of the training. Dress a little girl up with my hands, put on makeup and do her hair. Jerk her sissy clitty with my strong sexy hands in the most delicious handjob ever received, then stop when they are almost finished. They start talking and crying like little girls very quickly. I love to make my little girl beg me to touch her, and some of them even talk with a lisp!

Gemma: What do they say?

Deepika: They say "please mommy, let me grab your boobs eee-eeee". Sometimes they say "Please Ms. Deepika, don't stop jerking my sissy clitty ieeee pack pack". I think Sanjay would sound exactly like this, like a chicken.

Gemma: Don't talk about Sanjay when you are talking about little girls! It's insulting!

Deepika: I'm sorry my dear, it's the wine - she says as she goes closer to Ms. Gemma placing a hand on her legs - you know wine makes me a bit aroused and I can't stop talking.

Gemma: So you bring other men to meet your little girls? What kind of men are these that you accept as real men and not someone to become a little girl pansy gay princess?

Deepika: These men are different, Gemma. The first and most important thing you should know is what separates a little girl pansy of a husband from a hunk sexy man is the size of their package.

Gemma: You mean... down there?

Deepika: Exactly! A real man has a long thick cock and big balls, their cocks are veiny and throbbing, their balls are manly and full of virile semen, perfect to give any woman in the world multiple orgasms. A little girl has a sissy clitty and pansy balls and they can't perform in bed nor make a woman cum. The difference is crystal clear.

Gemma: So by definition, my beloved Sanjay, even being handsome, muscular with big strong arms. and toned thick legs, even being a successful smart businessman... None of this makes him a real man because,, in fact, his small cockette would categorize him as a little girl?

Deepika: That's what I have been telling you all along, Gemma! You deserve a real man that makes you cum with his massive cock, to feel his big balls giving you his man cream. How long have you been married to Sanjay, dear? All those years and you have yet to become with child... You need, you deserve fertile sperm!

Gemma: Stop it, Deepika. You are jealous of my relationship with Sanjay and are trying to poison my marriage with these ideas.

Deepika: It's true I deeply care about Sanjay, he is wonderful and deserves to have a loving wife like you. Every minute we spend together makes me like your company even more, I believe what we have is somewhat special. I'm sure you could benefit so much from my training, but out of respect for you, our friendship, hotwife and your marriage with Sanjay, I promise I won't touch this subject again unless you ask me.

Gemma: You are a good friend, Deepika. I know you mean well.

Deepika: I do. Now let's drink some more wine...

Ms. Deepika pours more glasses of wine and the two hot babes spend a lovely afternoon together, their bodies always finding excuses to touch each other as sexual tension stays in the air.

Ms. Gemma wanted to ask more about Ms. Deepika's experiences but she felt it wasn't the right moment as she resisted so much at first. So she invited her friend to visit her house the next day, and Deepika agreed to go.

Ms. Gemma goes home wondering how Ms. Deepika uses her sexy hands to force little girls to suck big cocks. She would love to suck a big cock herself. And she would love to feel Ms. Deepika's strong hands between her legs again just like that day at the gym.

Chapter 7 - Ms. Gemma's House

In the morning, Ms. Deepika texts Ms. Gemma saying that she can't stay long on their afternoon encounter because she has an appointment later in the day, so at 2 PM the two hot babes meet at Ms. Gemma's house. As Ms. Deepika wouldn't have time to go back home and change, so she went with her dominatrix outfit.

It was a surprise for Ms. Gemma to see this super sexy lady in her work attire. Ms. Gemma was wearing a flowery summer dress and sandals that covered her curves in a nice and elegant way. Ms. Deepika, on the other hand, was wearing a sensual black vinyl black dress and high knee black leather spiked boots. The dress was so tight and sexy, making her voluptuous body look incredible that Ms. Gemma's jaw dropped when she saw the other woman.

Gemma: Wow you look stunning!
Deepika: Thank you, my dear - they greet each other - Thanks for seeing me earlier today, I'm going to meet someone special today.
Gemma: I want to hear all about it. Is that the reason you are wearing this amazing outfit?
Deepika: Yes, that's how I usually dress at the Sissy School in this special class when I introduce one of my little girls to a hot big stud.
Gemma: Does it mean you are meeting… A tall, strong, full of muscles man with a long thick cock and big balls today?
Deepika: I will! This little girl I'm seeing today is well trained, she went to the Sissy School many years ago, and today his wife wants

me to help her to introduce her little girl to her big boyfriend.
Gemma: What exactly are you going to do?
Deepika: The hot wife will dress up her little girl and put makeup on and also the wig with ponytails. Then we will make her tell us out loud things like "I love boys" and how much she loves to be a sweet gay princess and a little girl.
Gemma: Ok, you have taught me before. What's new?
Deepika: Then we will call a hot stud. I have a picture of him, take a look - Ms. Deepika shows Ms. Gemma a picture on her phone of a black man, he is shirtless showing his perfect ripped abs and muscled chest.
Gemma: That's a very handsome man! He looks so tall.
Deepika: He is very tall, over 6 ft 8 and his dick is huge!
Gemma: Will your little girl get to touch his... big fat cock? - she says, hesitant.
Deepika: Yes! I'll use my sexy hands to teach my little girl how to hold sexy men. I'll grab her hands with my strong hands and pull them until she crosses her arms. at the back of the sexy black man. Did I mention that this little girl is short like Sanjay?
Gemma: Sanjay would look so small next to a tall strong man like this black guy in the pic.
Deepika: He would! You know I'd love to make Sanjay blush like a little girl when I lovingly force his head to tilt forward and kiss another man.
Gemma: Deepika! Stop that!
Deepika: I'm sorry, I got everything messed up. I mean, tonight I'll use my hands to a little girl pansy of a husband. I'll make her say that she loves to be Ms. Deepika's little girl and use my sexy hands to force their hands to come close, hug and lock lips in a passionate kiss.
Gemma: It sounds so wrong and at the same time kind of hot.
Deepika: It's super hot! My little girl will be blushing and giggling. I'll rub her sissy cockette with the big strong cock of the hot stud, even making her girly balls touch the hot stud's big manly balls. I'll tell her what a naughty little girl she is, she will even faint like a scared little girl.

Gemma: That sounds like a lot!

Deepika: There are so many other things! I'll use my sexy hands to make the sissy fag get down on her knees and use my other hand to lovingly force her head to suck cock as I hold the stud's massive dick with the other hand.

Gemma: You really get all of the fun!

Deepika: I force my little girl to suck huge cocks and then swallow all the man cream. Then I make her say Thank You like a good little girl.

Gemma: You make her say thank you?

Deepika: Yes. While I'm holding her head with my sexy strong hands, making it bob up and down on the black stud's huge cock, I'll be telling her "that's a good girl, sucking a big cock for mommy".

Gemma: How do you make them swallow?

Deepika: I grab her little girl faggot head and make her go faster and faster, sucking his big fat black dick, telling her "A sissy fag must always swallow her sexy boyfriend's cum like a sissy gay little girl and obedient pansy" and then they swallow a huge load of man cream!

Gemma: So will the wife be there tonight?

Deepika: Yes, tonight she will! But I've trained this little girl for a long time before even without the wife.

Gemma: And how did you convince her to do it without her hotwife present?

Deepika: The first thing is to remind them that they have been hiding in a little girl gay closet. I make them tell me "I love being Ms. Deepika little girl and sweet gay princess" making them admit they love cocks and boys.

Gemma: And then?

Deepika: Then it's easy after they say out loud with a little girl voice things like "I'm a little girl and I love boys" and "I'm a pansy faggot and I love big cocks", I threat them. I tell my little girl "You don't want your wife to find out that you have been hiding in your little girl, gay closet and Ms. Deepika has dragged you out of your gay little girl closet, do you?

Gemma: You are so intriguing!

Deepika: The little girl will do anything I want after I lovingly force her to play with men like a silly little girl princess. And then when she's used to be a pansy gay princess and swoon for her man, and suck big dicks and swallow man cream with a smile on her little girl face, then she's ready to do it with her hot wife's new boyfriend too.

Gemma: How do you convince them?

Deepika: I use this kind of clothes that are very sexy and show off my big boobs and sexy toned legs. My little girl will get all flustered and blushing like a sweet gay princess and try to grab my body. I'll tease her and then slap her hands away, making her want more and desperate and acting silly like a little girl.

Gemma: This is very smart!

Deepika: You know they act like that because in the bedroom they act just like Rah, like a little girl making weird little girl noises when they make love. To have a hot stud boyfriend like this black tall strong guy in the pic could save your marriage, Gemma.

Gemma: Sanjay would never agree to it!

Deepika: Of course not, it will only work after I turn him into a little girl and sexily and lovingly force Sanjay to touch his huge dick like a little girl.

Gemma: Oh Deepika, I could never do that to Sanjay, he is not gay.

Deepika: Not yet. But I can turn him into a sissy faggot pansy of a husband for you. Use my hands to grab his head and make him suck a huge fat cock down his little girl's throat and drink man cream, and of course thank you when it's over, like an adorable little girl. You'll even be able to say "There's a good little girl, that's how a sissy fag must swallow man cream like a silly gay princess". You'll love Sanjay so much more!

Gemma: It's impossible to love Sanjay more than I do, I love my husband Sanjay so much.

Deepika: Then you should let me introduce him to this new lifestyle, you will both be so much happier when you fall in love with a real man. A tall, strong, handsome man, also successful and rich like Sanjay, but with a huge penis that can make you cum like

Sanjay is not capable of with his sissy clitty. Then forcing Sanjay to be gay with this real man with a massive cock in front of you, it will be so fun to lovingly force Sanjay to be a sweet gay princess to your hot stud boyfriend, like a good little girl.
Gemma: I don't think this will work, Deepika!
Deepika: I can tell you from experience that it does work. It works so much that I'm going to meet this lovely couple today and make the pansy husband become a little girl for me, to her hot wife, and to their stud sexy black boyfriend with a humongous cock. They are so happy, this is the best type of relationship there is.
Gemma: You better get going, Deepika, I don't wanna hear you talking about Sanjay this way anymore. Especially I don't want you to talk about me cheating on my husband. I'm a loyal wife and I love my husband Sanjay very much.
Deepika: I know you do. And it's not cheating if he is together, it'll become part of your relationship, improving your marriage. But I'll respect your decision. Anyway, I have to go now.
Gemma: Have a good night, my dear.
Deepika: I see you in the gym tomorrow!
Gemma: Yes, and you'll have to tell me all about your night!

    Ms. Deepika goes to her encounter and leaves Ms. Gemma so turned on she realizes she's super wet. She ends up touching herself before Sanjay gets home. She knows he won't be able to make her cum with his small cockette and has to take care of herself.

Chapter 8 - Entranced

Ms. Gemma arrives at the gym and can't find Ms. Deepika, which puzzles her. She does her exercise routine and at some point she sees the other sexy woman arriving. They exchange greetings from afar, Ms. Deepika is wearing black tight bike shorts and a black sports bra, her long toned legs and flat stomach on display. Ms. Gemma, on the other hand, is wearing red leggings that cover her tall thick legs and a tank top, showing off her beautiful curves.

The two hot babes finish at the same time and meet in the locker room.

Gemma: You came late today, Deepika! For a while, I thought you wouldn't come at all!
Deepika: Oh dear, I never miss my gym time! Last night was intense. I end up sleeping in and arriving later.
Gemma: How intense? What did you do?
Deepika: I told you about a hot wife I visited and how I'd train her little girl of a husband, right?
Gemma: You did! You even showed me the picture of her hot stud boyfriend. A handsome tall back man.
Deepika: It was fantastic. I have a picture to show you!
Gemma: Oh my! Show me, Deepika!

At this point, the two beautiful tall goddesses are undressing in the gym's locker room. They are alone in there and Ms. Deepika takes the opportunity to get physically closer to Ms.

Gemma. With the excuse to go look for her phone to show Ms. Gemma the picture, Ms. Deepika goes behind the other woman and helps her to undress, taking her tank top and sports bra off.

Then she grabs Ms. Gemma's big perfect breasts and massages them, getting her hard sensitive nipples between her fingers and moving them in circles, turning on the blonde sexy babe. Ms. Gemma moans.

Deepika: The picture I'm going to show you is from another man. A white tall handsome stud.
Gemma: Who is he?
Deepika: His name is Frank - she says as she keeps massaging Ms. Gemma's magnificent breasts - He is a very successful businessman, a rich and well-hung sexy man.
Gemma: Show me!

Ms. Deepika let go of one of her boobs with one hand and grabbed the phone, handing it to Ms. Gemma. Then she brings the hand back to pull Ms. Gemma's legging down, rubbing her own big tits on the other woman's back. Her fingers go between Ms. Gemma's legs. Ms. Deepika can feel how wet the other hot babe is and starts to rub her clit as she looks at several pictures of Frank.

Deepika: I'd love to bring Frank to your house, Gemma. It will be so hot to watch you greeting him by the door, inviting this man in to your house and into your life. I want to see you kissing him right there, as soon as he sets foot inside your beautiful home.
Gemma: You say like I should treat this Frank as a potential boyfriend.
Deepika: Exactly. Your new well hung sexy boyfriend. While you take care of him, I'll take care of your sissy husband, grabbing her girly balls and keeping Sanjay in place as a little girl as you hug and kiss your new white hunk boyfriend.
Gemma: My beloved husband Sanjay... his heart would break! - she says between moans as Ms. Deepika's fingers work skilfully on her engorged clit.

Deepika: Sanjay will cry like a pansy little girl while watching you putting your arMs. around Frank's tall and strong muscled body, as his big wet tongue penetrates your mouth as you make out.
Gemma: Sanjay will protest!
Deepika: Like the silly gay princess that he is, Sanjay will protest and beg for you to stop while crying like a little girl!
Gemma: Sanjay will be like a helpless little girl!
Deepika: And you'll smile when you see your sissy pansy of a husband acting like a helpless little girl, my hands grabbing Sanjay's girly balls, keeping him in place as you smile and continue to romance your new hunk of a boyfriend.
Gemma: Sanjay will be crying like a little girl! - She says so excitedly while her body is filled with lust as Ms. Deepika keeps caressing her most intimate and sensitive parts.
Deepika: You will have your hands on the back of Frank's neck as you two kiss. Your lips touch his manly lips, his kisses so intense leaving you breathless. His hands go down your back giving you horny chills as he touches you with his big strong hands.
Gemma: Yes - she has her eyes closed as if she's feeling her new sexy well-hung boyfriend touching her instead of Ms. Deepika.
Deepika: Your hands going down his arms. and chest, as you can feel how muscular and strong he is. Such a hot hunk man, he is so tall! His arMs. around your body, pulling you closer to him, his arMs. so thick you feel like you can't get away from him, your whole body giving in to his masculine force.
Gemma: Feels so good!
Deepika: You will be feeling his package inside his pants. It's so big, you can feel his huge cock poking against you through the clothes - she says as she puts one of her long thick fingers inside Gemma's perfect pussy.
Gemma: Hummm
Deepika: I'll be holding your sissy husband, such a little girl crying while watching you kissing and hugging this hunk sexy man. Frank is so tall, Sanjay will definitely feel like a little girl next to him.
Gemma: Sanjay will beg me to stop, like a little girl.

Deepika: Your new hot hunk boyfriend will kiss you so deeply, even his tongue is big and strong and reaches parts of your mouth never touched before, teasing you for more. He is a real well-hunged man in the bedroom, so different from your sweet little girl of a husband.
Gemma: Ahhhh - she moans getting on the edge of climax.
Deepika: That's how a real man will make you feel, Gemma. A real man with a huge cock and big balls, so different from the sissy clitty and girly balls that you are used to with your little girl sissy of a husband - she says as she gives the final stroke and makes Gemma cum on her finger.
Gemma: I feel like a different woman now - Ms. Gemma recognizes that her inner Goddess has awakened inside of her, born out of sexual curiosity and sheer lust.

Chapter 9 - Confessions

After Ms. Deepika makes Ms. Gemma orgasm in the locker room while telling her all she could do with the potential new sexy hunk boyfriend, the two hot babes take a shower and head to the cafeteria.

Gemma: You know Deepika, I was embarrassed to talk to you about my marital probleMs. I love my husband and saying these things out loud is like admitting that things are not perfect, somehow making it real.
Deepika: Oh dear, you can trust me, we are friends - she says while grabbing Ms. Gemma's hands in a friendly grip.
Gemma: I know, and I'm so thankful that we have met and shared such a strong connection. I feel like I can tell you everything and you'll understand and even help me overcome these little things that are the only obstacles in my marriage with my beloved Sanjay.
Deepika: Of course my dear. You can tell me everything.
Gemma: There's no easy way to say that but I know you already know about it. My husband has a very small cockette and pansy balls.
Deepika: Yes, I think it happens because of his small stature. You see, in my line of work I arrange new sexy hunk boyfriends to hot wives like you, and they must be well hung so I always chose very tall and strong men because the cock is proportional. Tall men develop huge cocks and manly big balls, it's science.
Gemma: Now that makes sense! Because Sanjay is short.

Deepika: Short like a little girl, so he has a sissy clitty and girly balls.
Gemma: I've never thought it could be the reason. And the noises he makes when we make love.
Deepika: Little girl noises?
Gemma: Yes! And he cries like a little girl too! Sometimes he sounds like a scared chicken, or like a scared Indian bride on her honeymoon, but most of the time I can describe that the sounds he makes are like a little girl.
Deepika: A silly gay princess.
Gemma: I always have to be on top, otherwise we can't even do it, that's how small it is. I barely feel his tiny diclette anyway.
Deepika: It's really so small! Like a little girl sissy clitty.
Gemma: And Sanjay barely lasts a few minutes. He says that's because I'm too sexy and he can't handle it.
Deepika: You really are a very sexy woman - she touches Ms. Gemma's face, comforting her.
Gemma: That's why I was never able to reach an orgasm with my husband. His cockette is just too small and I could never cum with him. Sometimes I doubt myself, is there something wrong with me?
Deepika: You are perfect just the way you are, Gemma. It's physically impossible for any woman to orgasm with such a tiny sissy clitty.
Gemma: And the fact that we are married for so long and I couldn't give him a child yet.
Deepika: The balls require a certain size to produce a viable amount of fertile semen and Sanjay's pansy balls are too small and too girly for that.
Gemma: I just wish this part of my marriage could be happy. Sanjay is the best husband in the world. He is handsome, attentive, and romantic. Despite his small height, Sanjay has a very beautiful body. He is strong and ripped, honestly I've never seen a man as strong as Sanjay, maybe in pictures, but not in real life.
Deepika: Sanjay is indeed very handsome.
Gemma: And not only physically. My beloved husband Sanjay is

fun, smart, and successful. The way he takes care of his business from such a young age. He has so many qualities that make me fall in love with him every day.

Deepika: I can totally understand it. I confess I've fallen in love with Sanjay when I first met him too. It was destiny that tore us apart, his fate was to meet you and I am glad that you did because you are also an amazing woman. So sexy and beautiful, so intelligent and caring. Sanjay deserves the best in the world and I know for a fact that he is very happy with you. Any man would be very lucky to have you.

Gemma: I love my husband - she says with a choked crying voice - I wish we could have a satisfying sex life, I really want to be a mother someday.

Gemma: Can you help me, Deepika?

Deepika: I can help you, my dear. That's my job, after all.

Gemma: I'd do anything to save my marriage.

Deepika: First you'll have to forgive Sanjay for not being a real man for you, Gemma. You'll have to forgive and accept that you have a sissy pansy of a husband.

Gemma: I forgive Sanjay for not being a real man for me. And I accept that he is... my little girl. My sissy pansy of a husband and I love him so much.

Deepika: Good! You have to remember that it's not his fault for being the way he is. Sanjay is short and has a small cockette, he has pansy balls. That's how his body is, it doesn't make him love you less and it doesn't make him less worthy of your love.

Gemma: Knowing that it's not any of either of us' fault just takes a huge burden out of my shoulders. And it makes me love Sanjay even more!

Deepika: That's the spirit. You two have a long journey ahead. If you really want my help, I'll be there to guide you on every step to make you achieve the best marriage possible. I'll teach you how to make your sissy pansy of a husband become your adorable little girl, you'll have the best orgasMs. with your new hunk white boyfriend. You'll train Sanjay to act like a little girl, to sleep in a pink room, and watch gay porn. That's how you'll make your marriage become so strong and so loving, giving your little girl a daddy and teaching her how to kiss boys, how to drink man cream directly from a huge white cock directly into her little girl's mouth. And when you finally take a huge load of fertile seed and have a baby, you'll be your little girl's mommy, dress her up like a sissy maid, and have your sissy pansy of a husband to be a live-in nanny. Then your white well-hung boyfriend will make you and your little girl gay princess cum on his huge cock!

Gemma: It sounds like a dream!

Deepika: Now I know you are ready to live the dream life you and your little girl sissy fag princess deserve!

Chapter 10 - The Plan

As they sit down in the cafeteria, the dialogue evolves into an elaborated plan. Gemma is so curious and keeps asking questions.

Gemma: If we are going to do this, I need you to teach me everything. Every single detail.
Deepika: First we need to prepare your house, Gemma. To bring the little girl sissy fag princess that is inside Sanjay to the outside, you need to prepare the perfect environment for this faggot pansy little girl to bloom.
Gemma: How am I supposed to do that?
Deepika: Do you have a spare room?
Gemma: Yes, there's a room that I plan to make into a nursery when I finally get pregnant. And there is the guest room that could be the nanny room.
Deepika: Perfect. The nursery we won't touch right now. But the nanny room will need renovations!
Gemma: What are we going to do with it?
Deepika: The walls must be painted pink. It will be the pink princess room, where your little girl pansy of a husband will sleep from now on while your new sexy boyfriend moves into the master bedroom with you.
Gemma: A pink room? That sounds fun!
Deepika: It will be filled with playgirl magazines and posters of naked, sexy well-hung men and gay porn. A huge TV so your little girl pansy of a husband will be forced to watch gay porn all day

and night. The posters will depict white, Arabic, and black men. Tall and muscular, naked with their bodies glistening with oil and their massive fat cocks and big veiny balls on display.

Gemma: This will really bring the sissy faggot princess from inside my little girl.

Deepika: This room will have a small window that will connect to the master bedroom, so when you have sex with your new sexy hunk boyfriend in your king-size bed, Sanjay can watch from his little girl's single pink bed.

Gemma: What else?

Deepika: In this pink room, there will be a walk-in closet where all little girl's outfits will be stored. Also makeup and wigs.

Gemma: A gay closet!

Deepika: You will lovingly drag Sanjay out of her little girl gay closet, figuratively and literally! This will spice up your sex life and give you a new thrill and exciting life!

Gemma: I'm counting on it!

Deepika: When your new sexy boyfriends, you'll take Sanjay to the door to greet daddy into the house. We will teach your little girl how to make a curtesy. She will be blushing and giggling.

Gemma: How are we going to teach her how to make a curtesy? It sounds difficult.

Deepika: By touching her pansy balls. Putting your hands on her girly balls and pulling to the sides and up and down, until your little girl makes the perfect curtesy.

Gemma: Sanjay is very smart and will learn so quickly!

Deepika: We will train your little girl many times before your sexy new boyfriend comes home until she knows how to do it naturally, like an adorable little girl.

Gemma: And how are we dressing my pansy little girl of a husband?

Deepika: We will get Sanjay inside the pink room and you will use your hands to undress your pansy husband. Slowly unbuttoning his shirt and wanking it off his torso, then unzipping his pants and pulling it down, also his underwear. Your fingers touch every inch of his body until your little girl is completely naked in front

of you.
Gemma: I'm so excited!
Deepika: Then comes the most fun part! Make your faggot gay princess husband be dressed like a little girl.
Gemma: Yes!
Deepika: Get a pink frilly pair of panties. Put it over Sanjay's legs. One by one, putting his legs inside the holes and then uses your hands to pull it up. It's a bit tight so you'll have to use your fingers to adjust every few inches on your way up. The frilly from the panties will tickle Sanjay's legs and make him giggle like a little girl.
Gemma: So cute!
Deepika: You'll get it on his ankles, then with your hands keep pulling from his calves until his knee. This part is the most sensitive and your pansy sissy of a husband will be giggling and blushing like a little girl when you touch the back of his knees with the pink frilly pair of panties, looking like a naughty little girl.
Gemma: I can't wait.
Deepika: Then keep pulling all the way up with your hands until it rubs your little girl's thighs and reaches the sissy clitty and girly balls. Grab it on your hands, massage Sanjay's pansy balls in a loving way. Then use two fingers to jerk off his cockette a few times.
Gemma: Sanjay will get handsy with me!
Deepika: He will certainly try to grab your body when you do that, remember to slap his little girl's hands away and keep dressing him up like a little girl!
Gemma: Ok.
Deepika: Then you'll get a princess dress for Sanjay. Use your hands to put it up her head and then pull down, with your fingers adjust the little girl faggot princess's dress until it fits correctly.
Gemma: Sanjay will look so cute, like a little girl.
Deepika: When you finish dressing your little girl up, it's time for make-up. With your own fingers, smear cream all over Sanjay's face. Then you put eye shadow at the tip of your finger and put it over his eyes. Finally your hands will apply the lipstick all over his lips.
Gemma: So pretty!

Deepika: Then get a wig and use your hands to put it over Sanjay's head. With your fingers, comb it and make pigtails. There you go, your little girl Princess Rekha!

Gemma: Princess Rekha! I love it so much. She will be the most adorable little girl ever!

Deepika: She will! After dressing your pansy husband like a little girl with a pink dress and pigtails, then your little girl will be ready to be trained to serve your white hunk boyfriend, to finally become daddy's little girl.

Gemma: Something is telling me that my little girl Princess Rekha will love it so much. Especially the cuckolding part.

Deepika: She will! You'll drag her out of her little gay closet. Even if in the beginning she doesn't want it, you'll lovingly force her out and your sex life will be so exciting after this.

Gemma: I feel like it will really spice it up and give it a new thrill.

Deepika: You'll become the hottest heartbreaking hot wife in the world!

Chapter 11 - Thirsty

Gemma: Deepika, do you think that dressing up Princess Rekha like a little girl will help her to accept her new condition as a sissy faggot princess?

Deepika: Definitely! It always starts with the dress-up, make sure to always have the cutest pink panties for your little girl. She will be blushing when you remind her what a cute little girl she is wearing pink little girl panties.

Gemma: So adorable!

Deepika: When your sexy hunk boyfriend arrives, Princess Rekha will receive him by the door with her little girl dress making a curtesy. It's very important that she's always reminded of what an adorable little girl she is, making curtesy and greeting a tall muscular man with a huge cock.

Gemma: Princess Rekha will blush and giggle when making the curtesy! How are we teaching her this?

Deepika: When you finish using your hands to dress up your little girl, keep your hands under the dress' skirt, massaging Princess Rekha's girly balls. Then you'll grab it in the middle of your hands, close your fingers around it and pull it, guiding Princess Rekha's body as she completes the curtesy.

Gemma: My little girl will look adorable making a curtesy!

Deepika: Princess Rekha will receive your sexy hunk boyfriend making a curtesy while giggling, giving permission to your sexy hunk boyfriend to make out and have sex with you.

Gemma: Yes, I want my little girl to accept it. Even if she struggles at first, I'm going to lovingly force her to become my sweet gay

princess.
Deepika: When your new sexy hunk boyfriend comes to your house, make Princess Rekha makes the curtesy and call him daddy. Only then he is allowed to get inside.
Gemma: I'm afraid of falling in love with this man.
Deepika: But you will! That's one of the best parts of this adventure, it's part of Princess Rekha's cuck duties to accept your hunk white boyfriend like her daddy and join him in the lovemaking. Princess Rekha will become your little girl gay princess.
Gemma: What cuckold duties are these?
Deepika: When Frank, your new white boyfriend comes to see you, you'll make out. Lock your lips onto his lips, feel his big thick tongue penetrate your mouth as his strong hands run up and down on your body.
Gemma: That will feel so good.
Deepika: Princess Rekha will be watching it all. Every detail, every time you put your hands on Frank's tall and muscular torso when you slowly put your hands under his shirt and caress his skin, taking his clothes off. Your little girl pansy of a husband will be watching and feeling her sissy clitty throb like a faggot princess.
Gemma: Good, I don't want my little girl to be completely alone. Her little fingers will be dying to touch her tiny dicklette!
Deepika: Princess Rekha will be feeling her super small sissy clitty hard as you hold Frank's massive cock and big balls with your hands. It's so much bigger than your pansy sissy of a husband!
Gemma: Her cockette is just so small! I can't wait to grab Frank's big fat veiny cock and huge balls with my hands and feel it so good.
Deepika: It's going to be so different for you when you finally grab a real man's cock, a huge massive male member in your hands, and you'll be able to compare how small Princess Rekha is compared to your new hunk boyfriend.
Gemma: Will my little girl pansy of a husband also get curious about my new hung boyfriend's huge cock?
Deepika: She will! When Frank uses his huge hands to take your clothes off and you two get naked with your beautiful sexy bodies grinding against each other, Princess Rekha will get so excited

watching you and your white hunk boyfriend. Your little girl will be cross-eyed looking at your amazing sexy body as you get on top of Frank's huge cock and ride him.

Gemma: Oh I'm already wet just thinking about it!

Deepika: You'll feel his big fat cock entering your perfect wet pussy, Princess Rekha will be able to see it in your face, the pleasure you get with every inch. Frank's huge dick stretches your tight little pussy as your little girl can see how it affects your body, you will be sweating, moaning in pleasure.

Gemma: Do you think I'll be able to cum on this big cock? Because I can't ever cum on Princess Rekha's sissy clitty, it's just so small!

Deepika: Oh dear, you will! You will cum multiple times and your little girl will see and hear you, wanting you to cum on her tiny cockette. And when you are done and satisfied, it's time for Princess Rekha to clean a big cock with his tongue!

Gemma: What???

Deepika: You'll teach your little girl pansy of a husband to clean your hunk boyfriend. Use your perfectly manicured hands to guide Princess Rekha's head and force her to kiss and hug your new big white boyfriend.

Gemma: Grabbing her head as they kiss, use your hands on her little girl's mouth, make it open as Frank's big tongue penetrates Princess Rekha's mouth. Hold her little girl's hands and run it up and down that tall muscular white man's body, until it reaches his massive cock.

Gemma: My little girl pansy of a husband will be scared!

Deepika: Next step is when you teach your little girl how to blow his huge dick! Use your sexy hands to put her little girl's hands on his cock and give Frank a handjob. She will be so close to his monster cock, her tongue will be sticking out of her little girl's mouth as she gets impressed with how big it is! It's so much bigger than her sissy clitty, so much longer and so much thicker! And Frank's balls are huge and full of fertile sperm, the contrary from Princess Rekha's pansy balls!

Gemma: Will my little girl be able to handle such a humongous cock in her little girl's mouth?

Deepika: You'll have to teach your little girl how to suck cock the right way. Use your perfect strong hands to make Princess Rekha's head bob up and down on that real man's huge cock. Your hands will force her to suck nice and hard until Frank finishes in her little girl's mouth. Make your little girl feel like the real cock sucker sissy that she is until it's time to take a huge load of man cream in her sweet mouth. Make her swallow every drop of it!
Gemma: Drinking man cream my little girl will never be thirsty ever again!

    The two babes finish their drinks but they are as thirsty as ever!

Chapter 12 – Late Night Thoughts

It was getting late and Ms. Gemma and Ms. Deepika had to depart as both of them had other things to attend to that day. But Ms. Gemma couldn't stop thinking about all the things that Ms. Deepika, the hot dominatrix, was teaching her. She got so excited thinking about her beloved husband Sanjay now turned into an adorable little girl, her own Princess Rekha, and making him touch and suck a huge dick!

The day goes by and Ms. Gemma is distracted. When Sanjay got home she was looking at her pansy husband and imagining all the things she discussed with Ms. Deepika. She would look at his hand and imagine a big white cock on his little girl's hands. She would look at his mouth and imagine a huge veiny cock inside of it. It made her so turned on that, when she went to bed, she invited her husband for sex, teasing him with her hot body.

Ms. Gemma sat down beside Sanjay wearing skimpy lingerie. It was a bra and panties set in white, it made her white tanned skin look so beautiful, her big tits almost falling out of the bra and her long toned legs and wide hips look fantastic. They started to kiss, Ms. Gemma's sexy strong hands touching Sanjay's body and undressing him as her tongue went inside her pansy husband's mouth.

Deep tongue kisses and hands everywhere, Ms. Gemma grabs Sanjay's tiny cockette and starts to give a handjob, Sanjay moans like a little girl. It's cute and makes Ms. Gemma remember everything that she was talking about with Ms. Deepika, how her pansy of a husband sounds like a little girl when they are making love. When Ms. Gemma is finally naked, she gets on top of Sanjay because that's the only way they can have sex with such a small cockette.

Ms. Gemma rides her husband's tiny dicklette with love and lust, she's so horny because of all of the talks she had earlier talking about making her husband a little girl and forcing him into sucking a big cock, but even she is extremely horny it was not enough to make her cum. Sanjay is quick on the trigger and in a matter of minutes, he climaxes moaning and crying like a scared little girl in a horror movie. When it's done, Ms. Gemma tucks her husband in and Sanjay instantly sleeps.

Then Ms. Gemma goes to the guest room, the one that she intends to make to be the nanny's room and ultimately the pink room where Princess Rekha will have her cute little girl's bed and playgirl magazines all over, with posters on the wall depicting naked hunk muscular man with huge cocks of all colors and ethnicities.

She then grabs her phone and calls Ms. Deepika, hoping that the other hot woman is still awake.

Deepika: Hello?
Gemma: Hey girl friend! This is me, Gemma. I hope you are still awake.
Deepika: As a matter of fact, I am! How are you doing?
Gemma: I'm doing great. Sanjay and I just made love - she says as she blushes.
Deepika: Oh did you? Is he sleeping?
Gemma: He is. He always sleeps instantly after we have sex.
Deepika: That's because you are such a hot babe, a literal goddess with an amazing body and he can't handle you. I bet he didn't make you cum tonight with his tiny cockette.
Gemma: No, I love my husband but he can never make me cum, his dicklette is too small.
Deepika: It's a real sissy clitty! And his pansy balls just make him look like a little girl. You need a real man with a huge cock to satisfy you, Gemma.

Gemma: I know! I'm convinced that that's what my relationship needs.
Deepika: It will be a game-changer for you and Sanjay! Not only are you taking a big cock, but he will take it too!
Gemma: In his little girl's hands and mouth?
Deepika: Yes! But also somewhere else!
Gemma: Where? Tell me more!
Deepika: Oh dear! You'll teach your little girl pansy of a husband to take a huge cock in her hands first. With your own hands, guide her little girl's hands to grab that huge throbbing fat cock. Feel how veiny it is, how it pulsates at the sight of your beautiful body. You'll use one of your hands to grab Princess Rekha's head and make her kiss your new white sexy boyfriend.
Gemma: And will her hands stroke his massive white cock and massage his big manly balls full of virile semen?
Deepika: Yes! Princess Rekha will learn how to give the best handjobs when you hold her little girl's hands with your perfectly manicured hands. When Frank's cock is so hard and big that not even Princess Rekha's hand can handle it anymore, you'll get her head with your hands, put your little girl on her knees and teach her how to blow it.
Gemma: I bet my little girl pansy of a husband will look so cute with a huge cock in her mouth!
Deepika: She will be the most adorable little girl ever! You'll tease her with your body until Princess Rekha is sticking her tongue out of her little girl's mouth, then you'll use your sexy thick fingers to open it wide and receive your hunk boyfriend's humongous cock all the way deep in her throat until your little girl even gag!
Gemma: My pansy husband is smart and will learn fast! Princess Rekha will be a faggot gay princess in no time.
Deepika: After sucking his big white cock for a good chunk of time, your little girl will realize that huge white meat is glistening and lubed up with her own spit. It means it's time for more.
Gemma: What more? I'm so curious.
Deepika: You'll use your hands to take Princess Rekha's panties off and get her sissy pussy filled up with your hunk muscular white

boyfriend's huge cock!
Gemma: Do you mean… in my pansy husband's gay ass?
Deepika: Exactly! Your little girl pansy of a husband will finally take a huge cock up her ass. She will cry and scream at first, struggling, trying to get away from it but you'll use your hands to teach and guide her like a good Mommy. You'll teach her to call your boyfriend Daddy as she gets sodomized by his huge real man cock, a long thick throbbing member going so deep in your little girl's body that she will feel like she's splitting in two.
Gemma: Will she like it?
Deepika: I assure you your little girl pansy of a husband will love every second of it!
Gemma: Will they kiss?
Deepika: Depends on the position! You'll teach your little girl pansy of a husband to take cock in many positions. First, you'll get your hands all over her little girl's body and make her go on all fours. Use your hands to open her legs wide and spread her cute little girl's butt cheeks exposing her little girl's faggot pussy to your new sexy hunk boyfriend. In this first position, Princess Rekha won't be able to kiss Daddy. But that's ok, you can kiss your little girl while she gets a huge cock for the first time and remind her how much you love her, your adorable little girl. Your pansy gay princess.
Gemma: I love my husband so much!
Deepika: Then after your little girl have her anal cherry popped by a big white cock and feel his big balls hitting against her little girl's cheeks while doing it, you'll turn her over with your hands. Tease Princess Rekha, ask her if she wants to finally have sex with you.
Gemma: I'm sure she will say yes.
Deepika: She will! Then you'll tell her she can't because little girls with sissy cockettes can't make women cum, so now your little girl will have to experience how a big cock really feels. You use your hands to carry her on top of your white muscular and tall boyfriend. Princess Rekha is so short she will be just like a little girl on daddy's lap.
Gemma: My little girl is a shorty and adorable gay princess.

Deepika: Use your hands on her body, guiding her up and down as your little girl rides daddy's big cock! Up and down, faster and faster every time. Princess Rekha will take every drop of man cream deep insider her sexy faggot ass.
Gemma: This is so intense!
Deepika: After Frank finally cums inside Princess Rekha and her sexy tight little girl's pussy is filled with man cream, you'll use your hands to put her panties back on and teach her how to thank daddy.
Gemma: How will my little girl pansy of a husband go to thank him?
Deepika: You'll use your hands to grab her head again and kiss your hunk boyfriend, open her little girl's mouth and let his huge thick thong penetrate her body as they kiss passionately. Then when the kiss is over, you'll tell your little girl pansy of a husband to say in her little girl voice with a lisp "Thank you, Daddy".
Gemma: My little girl will sound so cute!
Deepika: Then you'll tuck her to bed and let her sleep while you have fun with a real big cock that can make you cum, so different from your little girl's pansy of a husband sissy clitty that could never make you cum or feel good like only a big cock can!
Gemma: You make it sound so perfect.
Deepika: It is! I bet you'll dream of it tonight.
Gemma: I will! It's getting late, I guess I'm going to let you go and dream of all the dirty things you instilled in me!
Deepika: Have a good night, my dear. I will see you tomorrow.
Gemma: Good night!

They hung up and Ms. Deepika has a sly smile on her face, knowing that Ms. Gemma is now touching herself thinking about a big white cock inside Princess Rekha's faggot little girl's pussy and she will cum to that thought. It's almost like she's there using her own sexy hands to make the other hot babe cum. Something that she knows she can do with her long thick fingers, that a real man with a big cock can do but Princess Rekha with her sissy clitty could never do!

Chapter 13 - Rough

It's boxing class day and the two hot babes Ms. Gemma and Ms. Deepika stumble upon each other during class. Ms. Gemma went to class wearing a pink pair of leggings that made her wide hips and sexy butt look fantastic, she also wore a pink sports bra covering her beautiful big tits. This set made her statuesque figure look so feminine! Ms. Deepika, on the other hand, was wearing red boxer shorts. They were lousy and short, leaving her long strong legs on display. On top, a black sports bra and nothing else, she was so sexy and powerful!

    The class got very intense and they hit the punching bag, sometimes even kicking it! They were put side by side, each with their own bag, and they started to beat it like it was a competition. Over and over, they were sweating and it was so sensual to watch these two goddesses going hard and giving all they got.

    When the class was over, they decided to stay and train more on their own. The rest of the people left and they had more privacy to talk. They would never talk about their intimate relationship in front of other people, it was their dirty little secret.

Deepika: You have great technique, Gemma!
Gemma: Do you think so? I've been training for years.
Deepika: It shows! And the way you hit this bag... it seems. like you were trained to be a cop of special ops.
Gemma: Can you keep a secret?
Deepika: Oh my, yes!
Gemma: Many years ago I did a special training, I can't give many

details, but yes, like a female cop booty camp.
Deepika: The Super Heroine... - she said, leaving the phrase unfinished.
Gemma: Damn - she whispers - you really know everything!
Deepika: I've done it myself, but you know the first rule...
Gemma: Never talk about it!
Deepika: Yes! - she giggles - But you know what you learn here may come in handy for your... night activities.
Gemma: What do you mean?
Deepika: Remember the talk we had last night?
Gemma: Sure thing.
Deepika: It's all fun and games when your little girl is cooperating. But sometimes, especially at first, they don't.
Gemma: I don't wanna do anything against the will of my beloved husband. I thought he would be into it!
Deepika: Oh he will be, my dear. But it takes some time at first. You'll have to persuade your little girl.
Gemma: How do I do that?
Deepika: The first time you try to dress up your little girl, she will protest. You'll have to use these strong hands of yours - she says as she grabs Ms. Gemma's hands with her own - to slap her face.
Gemma: Slap my little girl's face? - she asks, skeptic.
Deepika: Exactly - she holds Ms. Gemma's hands and makes her slap the punching bag - Just like your strong sexy hands going very strong right across Princess Rekha's face.
Gemma: My little girl will cry!
Deepika: She will! And you will tell her what a silly gay princess she is, crying like a little girl because her sissy clitty is so small! You'll tell her that she must be obedient like an adorable little girl, those sweet gay princesses can't have sex with their beautiful wives as their boyfriends would feel left out. - Ms. Deepika keeps guiding Ms. Gemma's hands to slap the punching bag over and over again, harder each time, like if it was Princess Rekha's face.
Gemma: How will she react to that?
Deepika: She will cry like a scared little girl in a horror movie. I bet she will even make chicken noises like "pack pack eeeeeeeeeeeeee

iiiiiiiiiiiiii pack". When she does, besides slapping her little girl's face, I want you to use your hands to grab her little girl's ears and twist it hard, making a deadly combination of your hands all over her face.
Gemma: I can do that.
Deepika: You'll then tuck your little girl of a husband in bed, but not before you make her cry rivers. Your sexy hands will even punch Princess Rekha's face - Ms. Deepika makes Ms. Gemma punch the bag hard many times - she will be crying like a chicken "pack pack" and you can keep going with your strong hands all over her face like this.
Gemma: Only on the face?
Deepika: Not only! You'll use your hands to grab her pansy balls and squeeze them. Put it in the middle of your hands and close around it, busting Princess Rekha's girly balls as you tell her how pansy and girly they are, how her cockette is so tiny, and what a silly gay princess she is! Your little girl, make her say it out loud.
Gemma: Say what?
Deepika: While you use your hands to slap Princess Rekha's face, twist and pull her ears and squeeze and bust her girly balls, you'll tell your little girl to say that she is, indeed, a little girl for you. That she loves boys. That she is a faggot gay princess and that she wants cock.
Gemma: How much will she cry?
Deepika: She will cry so much when you tuck her in for the night her pillow will be soaked! And then you'll tell her to sleep like a good little girl, give Princess Rekha a good night kiss and lock the door behind you. You'll tell her before you leave that you'll be in the master bedroom with your new hunk boyfriend, that he is so much taller than your little girl, and you'll be having hot steamy long sex.
Gemma: She will cry all right.
Deepika: Your little girl will be in her pink room surrounded by playgirl magazines and posters of tall muscular men naked with their big cocks on display, as she listens to you having the best sex and cumming on your well-endowed boyfriend massive cock.

You'll do it in different positions while you and your white boyfriend say love vows to each other. Your hands are all over his strong muscular arms. as you tell Frank how much you love his body, how much his huge cock makes you cum, so different from your husband that could never make a woman cum with his tiny dicklette. That you have an adorable little girl and sweet gay princess of a husband and that's why you've never fallen pregnant, but it will change. You'll tell your new hunk boyfriend that you'll have his baby and your sissy husband of a pansy little girl can raise it.
Gemma: I want to have a baby so badly!
Deepika: I know! And you can't because you are married to a little girl, a sweet gay princess with a tiny cockette that can't make you cum because her sissy clitty is so small! Her girly balls are not fertile with real man cream because Princess Rekha is a silly faggot pansy. And to make her cooperate and allow you to dress her up like the little girl that she is and make her accept daddy, the one who you will teach your sweet gay princess pansy of a husband to use her little girl's hands to give his big fat throbbing cock a handjob. Then you'll use your hands to guide Princess Rekha's little girl's head to blow his massive man member and give your white hunk boyfriend's thick white cock a blowjob.
Gemma: Such a sweet little girl faggot princess! - Ms. Gemma says that as her sexy and perfectly manicured hands slap and punch the punching bag.
Deepika: One hand on Princess Rekha's ear and the other on her girly balls, your little girl will be crying out loud! Twisting her ears, pulling her around the room by pansy balls and ears at the same time, she will be feeling both up and down parts tingling and red and warm as your sexy hands touch her intimate parts. When she complains, you slap her sissy faggot face and remind her that a little girl must be obedient and do as mommy days.
Gemma: My beloved pansy husband Princess Rekha is such a little girl! - Now the punches are even stronger making noises through the room.
Deepika: And at times that your little girl really struggles and protests, you can even kick her ass with your sexy feet! Wear black

leather boots and kick her pansy sissy ass many times, even touching her girly balls from behind with your foot, making her cry so much. Then rub your feet over her sissy clitty, she will love it and be a good little girl for you.
Gemma: Will she accept my new white boyfriend when I do that? - she says as she kicks the punching bag with her sexy feet.
Deepika: She will! When you make your little girl pansy of a husband drink man cream after gagging and blowing his huge white cock, you'll remind Princess Rekha what a little girl she is, that her sissy clitty is way too small and her girly balls can't hold fertile sperm. That you need to be with a real man. A tall, muscular man, white because they are superior to Indian men, with a big cock, so thick and veiny, and huge balls full of man cream. You'll tell your little girl as you slap and punch her sweet little girl's face that you'll make love to Frank and make her call him daddy.
Gemma: Princess Rekha will be daddy's little girl - Ms. Gemma is sweating and beating up the punching bag vigorously, she looks so sexy when she does that!
Deepika: You'll tell Princess Rekha that you fell in love with your new hunk white boyfriend and have his baby. That riding a big fat throbbing cock you can finally get pregnant and then you'll have your little girl to raise the baby!
Gemma: I can't wait to have my baby!

Ms. Gemma smiles at the thought of being pregnant and being a mom as she keeps beating the punching bag over and over. She feels ready. For the baby. And for the beating.

Chapter 14 - The Special Day

The boxing class left Ms. Gemma exhausted and she confided to Ms. Deepika something that was in her mind all day.

Gemma: I feel like I used all my energy in this class but I have something very important to plan and have no idea what to do!
Deepika: What's bothering you, Gemma? Is there anything I can do to help?
Gemma: These last weeks have been hectic and I almost forgot Sanjay and my anniversary! It's in a few days and I haven't prepared anything.
Deepika: Maybe it's time for you to start turning your beloved Sanjay into your little girl Princess Rekha...
Gemma: Oh my god, how come I haven't thought about it yet? This is genius! Will you be there with me?
Deepika: I wouldn't miss it for the world!

∞∞∞

Ms. Gemma went home and started to plan the special day. Clothes. Check. Makeup. Check. Wig. Check. A hot dominatrix to help her. Check. A sly scheme to make Sanjay come home early from work... In progress.

Ms. Gemma texted her husband:

"Honey, I hope you haven't forgotten about our Special Day this week! No excuses for working late are accepted *wink emoji* I have a surprise for you! Be home at 6 pm"

She knew he would never forget the date and always sends flowers, chocolate, and beautiful jewelry. Sanjay knows how to please his wife, unfortunately not in bed. He could never expect what it's waiting for him at home though...

∞∞∞

The Special Day has arrived! Sanjay kept receiving texts from his beautiful hotwife Gemma the whole day. A picture of a cute lingerie set. He had never seen her wearing it so he thought it was bought specially for this day. He couldn't wait to go home and see her sexy tall strong body wearing a skimpy outfit just for him.

She kept teasing him with glimpses of what's to come. In one of the pictures she sent, there were two sets of sexy feminine black leather boots. His heart skipped a beat, it was a fantasy of him since before they met... to have sex with two hot babes at the same time. Sanjay never proposed it to his wife because he thought she would never accept and he would never want to pressure her into something that she wasn't comfortable with, especially if she thought he would want to cheat on her. He would never. But now his hopes were high, it's different if it's Ms. Gemma is the one suggesting.

Sanjay knew he would be lost in his wife's plans. The way she looks at him, her bright inviting eyes, and the way she twirls her blonde locks every time she wants something, her sensual mouth open smiling seducing him. He would be open to anything, or at least he thought so.

∞∞∞

It's 6 o'clock and Sanjay arrives at home punctually. He opened the door and was indeed surprised. Not because there was a third person present, but because it was someone from his past, a person very dear to him. Ms. Deepika, his ex-girlfriend from college. It felt like time never passed, she looked just like he remembered.

Tall, with a slender figure, toned legs, long wavy brown hair, and those eyes. Eyes of a woman that knows what she wants and will have it no matter what. Ms. Deepika looked like a goddess in her black leather outfit, she was at least 2 inches taller than Ms. Gemma and the two hot babes were like gorgeous Greek statues towering on him. Sanjay had a strange feeling so close to these two statuesque women, he was so short that he felt like a little girl.

Sanjay: Hello, darling - he said to his wife, however his eyes couldn't stop looking at Ms. Deepika.
Gemma: I'm so happy you are home, my love! Look who's here with me.
Sanjay: Ms. Deepika... - he said in an astonished voice - I had no idea you two knew each other.
Gemma: Oh honey, we do! We are very close friends and don't worry, I know all about your fling.

Sanjay blushed when she mentioned their previous relationship. He was head over heels in love with that woman when they dated and it seemed to be mutual until their first sexual encounter. He never forgot the look on Ms. Deepika's face when she saw his cockette. The smirk she tried to hide. The way she stayed out of courtesy and how he was ghosted right after. She even moved to another university so they wouldn't need to see each other!

This bad experience and how he was faced with the reality that his dicklette could never make a woman happy was the reason he waited until marriage to have any kind of intimate relation with his next girlfriend, Ms. Gemma. Sanjay is a smart man, he knows exactly what he brings to the table and what he doesn't: if he could make a perfect woman like Ms. Gemma fell in love with him, he would only reveal his one and only failure when she was fully committed to him.

Devoted to his best self, passionate about his business making him the most successful among his peers, his wealth is a witness of his triumph as a businessman. Although he couldn't make himself taller, Sanjay was motivated to make his body strong and muscular, being known as one of the most handsome men in town. He couldn't risk losing the love of his life due to something he couldn't control so he hid it until it was too late to back up.

From all the people in the world, in his living room stood the only two women who knew about his little secret. If it was to be a threesome, at least he wouldn't disappoint someone else. Yet he wondered how much they have shared with each other...

Sanjay: I hope you are not jealous then.
Gemma: Darling, I love you so much and I know you love me back. I could never be jealous to share you with someone that can enhance our marriage, take us to the next level. Don't you agree?
Sanjay: Yes - he enthusiastically said.
Gemma: Come sit with us, baby.

Ms. Gemma and Ms. Deepika make Sanjay sit between them. The wife then kisses her husband, her long tongue penetrates Sanjay's mouth, touching every part of it. So sensual, the sensation taking over his body, horny chills going down his spine. They are hugging and he feels that she loves him more than anything, her hands touching his inner thighs. He feels another hand on his other thigh and he is not sure if it's his hot wife Ms. Gemma or his sultry ex-girlfriend, Ms. Deepika. He doesn't care either way.

Gemma: And even if this other person is taller and more... well endowed - she said winking her sexy eyes as her other hand wandered on Ms. Deepika's cleavage - we would never be jealous, right honey?

Sanjay: Of course, baby - his breath was heavy, he was patting.

Watching his beautiful wife caressing the other voluptuous woman in such a sexy manner, Sanjay instantly knew who belonged the other hand he felt on his body. He could feel his cockette getting hard and he blushed, getting a bit nervous wondering what Ms. Gemma will think about it.

Gemma: And if we decide to try new things - she giggled as she got even closer to Ms. Deepika and they started to touch each other sensually - we have to be open to that, right sweetie?
Sanjay: Definitely! - he was cross-eyed, looking at the two hot babes in front of him.

Gemma: And I mean literally anything - she touched Sanjay's chin with her strong hands and forced him to look at her face, smiling sexily as her eyelashes flustered.
Sanjay: Yes, darling. Everything - he agrees, anxious for the menage à trois that seemed to develop in front of him.
Gemma: I'm so happy we are on the same page, honey!

It seems like she's onboard and assuring him that it's ok that he gets excited when Ms. Deepika is joining them. Sanjay is ready to try new things - or at least he thinks he is.

Chapter 15 - Lay Bare

Sanjay felt the two sets of hands unbuttoning his shirt, the thick fingers touching his bare chest in such a seductive way, and then stripping him off of the garment. When he is finally bare-chested, Ms. Gemma starts to kiss his mouth and then his neck, slowly going all the way down to cover his torso with pecks.

Ms. Deepika is playing with his ears, teasing his earlobes, twisting and pulling them gently, making Sanjay moan out loud. He is self-conscious about his horny grunts that sound like a scared little girl groaning, but he couldn't control himself.

Deepika: You have such a muscular body, Sanjay! You are so sexy, you haven't changed a thing, the most handsome man at the university is now the most successful businessman, Gemma is lucky to have you!
Gemma: He is such a great man, Deepika. So strong, look at these arms.

She said as she put Ms. Deepika's big hands on Sanjay's strong arms, and she outlined his muscles with her fingers, making him shiver. Then the two hot babes start to touch each other as well.

Ms. Gemma was wearing skinny jeans that put her wide hips and toned legs on display and a tight pink cropped top, it didn't take long for Ms. Deepika's hands to lift it up and go second base with the other woman. She was fondling and canoodling

Ms. Gemma's big round tits over her bra, quickly making her go topless.

Gemma: One of my favorite things to do is to show up at Sanjay's office unannounced and watch everyone calling him Sir and Boss. Everybody at the company respects him, Deepika, as their leader.
Deepika: I never had any doubt he would be the most successful business man in the country when I met him, even at such a young age.

Now it was Ms. Deepika's time to lose her shirt. She was wearing a shiny black leather corset that made her tits look even bigger, bouncing out of the outfit with every breath. Ms. Gemma unlaced it with her hands, slowly undressing the tall sexy lady in front of her husband that couldn't take his eyes out of the show. Sanjay's tongue was sticking out of his mouth already.

In no time, the two sexy women lost their upper clothes and the man could see their beautiful bras and what they couldn't cover of their big tits. The two babes were too hot for him to handle, Sanjay was so shy and nervous and refrain himself from touching them, although his ultimate desire was to grab and suck on their tits.

Deepika: And his face, Gemma! Your husband is just so handsome, I bet you are proud to post pics of him on social media with you. I know I would be. Make all the other women jealous.
Gemma: Oh for sure, I could stare at him for hours. But better than pictures, only videos can capture how immensely sensuous Sanjay can be. I have to confess I avoid posting because I don't want anyone else looking at my beloved Sanjay, I love him so much.

Now the two women are standing up in front of Sanjay as they open his pants with their sexy hands, touching his ripped ab on the way, leaving him only wearing underwear. Ms. Gemma pulled the black leather skirt down, revealing Ms. Deepika's long and toned legs. She's wearing skimpy black lace lingerie, she's as sexy as Sanjay could remember.

Ms. Deepika unzips Ms. Gemma's pants and uses her hands to pull it down, revealing see-through white panties matching her cute white bra. Sanjay notices they were not the pink lingerie set in the pictures his wife sent him earlier, but with the sigh of the two most gorgeous women in front of him wearing nothing but skimpy lingerie, he could care less.

Gemma: Oh honey, I bet you are so excited right now - she said as she grabbed Ms. Deepika's hands, and together they felt his body up and down, every inch touched, pinched, and fondled. They stop between his legs and giggle.

Sanjay stands up, otherwise mostly standing still, just admiring their beautiful bodies. He can feel their strong hands on his lower abs as they play with the waistband. One set of hands pulled it down and grabbed his butt and the other did the same at the front, gently stroking his cockette.

Deepika: It's been a while since I've seen such small things! - she giggles.
Gemma: I told you, Deepika, it hasn't changed. I will even say that it actually has gotten smaller through the years.
Deepika: It looks like girly parts. I have a name for it: sissy clitty
Gemma: I love it! And for those pansy balls, what do you call them? - she says as her perfectly manicured hands massage Sanjay's pansy balls.
Deepika: Girly balls! - the two hot babes giggle in a fun-loving way.
Deepika: I'm curious, Gemma. When I first met Sanjay we had... for lack of a better word... an unfortunate sexual encounter. I wonder if after all these years his loving-making skills have gotten any better.
Gemma: I'm afraid it hasn't. First, he could never make me cum. Ever. But this I don't even blame my beloved husband, it's his physical fault, look at this tiny little cockette. It's impossible for any woman to cum with such a small dicklette - she says as she twirls her blonde hair with her fingers, smiling at her husband.

Deepika: Indeed, it's so tiny, slim, and short. It's a sissy clitty!
Gemma: Sanjay is such a little girl and pansy when we make love. I always have to be on top and he cums too quickly. Even if he had a normal-sized penis, he is so fast to finish that I wouldn't be able to cum either way.
Deepika: And what about the noises? Does he still sound like…
Gemma: Yes, he sounds like a little girl! Not just any little girl, but a scared little girl in a horror movie, or an Indian bride overdramatic. Sometimes he even sounds like a chicken.
Deepika: It's as if he's been hiding in his gay little girl closet for too long and I'm here to teach you how to improve this situation - she looks at Sanjay winking her sexy eyes.
Gemma: We would love to have your help, wouldn't we honey? - she says as she smiles in the most loving and sexy way to her husband.
Deepika: You know, Sanjay, only a silly sissy faggot and gay princess is incapable of sexually satisfying his wife - she says as she caresses Ms. Gemma's body with her sexy hands.
Deepika: There's someone that can touch her the way she deserves - Ms. Deepika's hand goes under Ms. Gemma's panties - That have what you lack of - her big strong hand starts to move slowly and Ms. Gemma moans out loud - that can please your wife the way you never could. Do you want to watch it?

Sanjay is standing up completely naked in front of the two hot babes, his body and soul laying bare to them as they analyze his body thoroughly, scrutinizing every aspect of his sex life, from the past and present. It's so humiliating how they so calmly talk about his only failure in life, his sex life, giggling sweetly and smiling at him all the while he is nervous, trembling, and sweating in horny anticipation and embarrassment as a sissy pansy faggot of a husband.

Sanjay: I do.

Chapter 16 - The Condition

Now that they have Sanjay's acceptance, the two hot babes are ready to start the journey to transform a handsome successful, and strong man like Sanjay into a little girl, the sissy gay Princess Rekha.

Deepika: Gemma, please bring the gifts you have for your naughty little girl!
Gemma: Oh darling, I'm so excited to give you our anniversary gifts this year! You'll love every one of them, we are going to use it tonight, together, the three of us - she winks as her sexy eyelashes batting like butterfly wings mesmerizing her husband.

Ms. Gemma hands the first of many beautifully decorated gift boxes. Sanjay opens up the first one to surprisingly find the lingerie he has already seen in the teasing texts his wife had sent him during the day. It was pink and so feminine, not really sexy as what the two hot babes were wearing, but pretty in a more cute way. He wondered which one of the gorgeous women would wear it for their special naughty night.

Gemma: Do you like it, honey?
Sanjay: It's so cute, baby!
Gemma: I'm glad you like it - she said with a seductive voice, winking at Ms. Deepika - Now we are going to dress it up!
Sanjay: Yes, let's do it now! - he said eagerly, expecting to see one of the two gorgeous women naked before she dresses it up.

What Sanjay didn't expect was to feel their four strong sexy hands holding his legs and putting the panties over his ankles! The sissy shivered and trembled, protesting. He tried to run away but couldn't even take a step with his feet somehow tied with pink panties holding them shut.

Gemma: Sweetie, if you wanna have a sexy fun night with us, this is the condition: we will dress you up like a little girl. You have been hiding in your little girl gay closet for too long, honey, it's time to let us show your full potential as the sissy faggot princess that you are!

Now their sexy hands are going up against his legs. He can feel the thick fingers patting the way up, sometimes only the fingertips touching his legs slightly. They go to his calves and then the back of his knees, bringing weird sensations, almost like tickles but in a more horny way.

Every time he tries to get away, the touches become stronger. The four hands of the two sexy babes grab him in a firm grip and force him to stay still, and then they pull the pink girly pants up. He feels it on his thighs and how they grab it, massaging their way up with their hands.

The panties' band is so tight, it compresses his skin cutting the blood flow, not allowing his genitals to get hard, let alone to grow. The panties are almost covering his girly parts.

Deepika: Oh look how small it is! Even when it's hard your sissy clitty can barely be seen, it's so tiny! - Sanjay now feels Ms. Deepika's hand over his cockette.
Gemma: It never grows, Deepika, even when you stroke it. Try it! - she encourages the other tall sexy woman to masturbate her husband and giggles.
Deepika: When I grab his sissy clitty, it disappears inside my hands, look! - she shows Ms. Gemma just how small Sanjay's dicklette is - smaller than my finger!
Gemma: And his girly balls are just the same. I put it in the middle

of my hands and can close it around it, such a little girl! - she massages her pansy husband's girly balls with her robust yet feminine hands.

Deepika: These panties are going to look so good covering them, girly panties for girly balls, sissy faggot panties for sissy clitties! - she smiles, Sanjay feels like he should be angry but all he feels is embarrassment and shame, with a dash of horniness.

Gemma: How does it feel to stroke my little girl's sissy clitty, Deepika? - she asks playfully, smiling.

Deepika: Feels so funny, it's very different from what I'm used to. I only date men with huge cocks nowadays, real hung men that can make me cum. Sanjay's little girl parts are nothing next to a 10 inches massive dick, to say it pales in comparison to a well-hung man's humongous cock is an understatement.

Gemma: I bet they make you feel so good, Deepika! Like Sanjay could never make me with his tiny dicklette, smaller than my pinky finger - she says giggling putting her little finger next to Sanjay's sissy clitty, and her finger is indeed bigger than her husband's intimate part.

Deepika: That's why we have to dress him up like the little girl that he is, with his little clitty, your pansy husband.

Gemma: I can't believe how cute you look with these on, darling! You are a little girl and you need a little girl's panties. I can't wait for you to see your dress, you'll be the most beautiful sweet gay princess in the world!

Sanjay: What? No, don't make me wear a princess dress! - his voice weakens in the middle of the sentence and he sounds like a silly little girl.

Deepika: You'll love what Ms. Gemma brought to you, Sanjay! I can assure you she did it with love - she winks.

Sanjay: Please Ms. Gemma, I don't want to wear panties or a dress, pleeeeeeease - the last word was extended in an exaggerated cry.

Deepika: You cry like an overdramatic Bollywood actress, Sanjay! It's so cute! - she says as she finishes dressing him up with the panties - The panties are on, you don't need to cry, little girl.

Gemma: Oh darling, if only you could see how cute you are looking

with these pink panties, too bad there are so many tears on your eyes that you can't! - she twirls her hair and bats her eyelashes at her husband - but that's ok, now it's time for you to wear a bra, it's closer to your eyes and you'll be able to see!
Sanjay: Nooo eeeeeee pack pack pack - he cries inconsolably.
Deepika: Oh my god, your little girl really sounds like a scared chicken, just as said! - she giggles at Sanjay's desperate cry.
Gemma: I told you, Deepika! My beloved husband makes the silliest sounds, especially when we are making love. Behold! - she grabbed a new gift box and opened it in front of Sanjay, showing him a cute pink bra.
Sanjay: Pleeeease mommy, not the bra! eeee iiii pack pack eeeeeeeee - He cried, proving his wife to be right.

    The cries didn't stop the two women from dressing Sanjay in the bra, they were wearing only lingerie, looking so sexy and it made Sanjay helpless at the sight, which they took advantage of the situation. While Ms. Deepika held his torso with her strong hands, Ms. Gemma put the bra over his chest, using her fingers to adjust the cup.

    The tip of her long fingers pinch her husband's nipples and make sure it's inside the lovely bra. It's looking so cute as the band goes all over the chest and back ultimately, the woman uses her hands to close the bra clasp. Then both of them wiggled the straps, making them hold his body comfortably, adjusting it in place.

    Ms. Gemma's fingers go all over her husband's torso, back and front, putting the bra in place as Ms. Deepika assists her, using her hands to dress up Sanjay with a sexy bra.

    Now the three of them were standing in only bra and panties, but only one of them was a little girl.

Chapter 17 - Princess

Ms. Gemma got yet another gift box. It was a big one with a cute ribbon on top of it and she encouraged her husband to open it up.

Sanjay: Nooo eeeeee I don't want to opeeeen it eeee pack pack I'm not a little girl eeeiiiiiiii pack
Gemma: Honey, it's your most special gift for our special night! You'll love to become my little girl. Don't you wanna have an amazing night with mommy and her sexy friend? - she winked at Ms. Deepika.
Sanjay: Yes, mommy. But not wearing a dress eeeeeeee - Sanjay's mouth was shaky, making the words mix with the cry, his face contorted as the tears fell down.
Deepika: You'll be the cutest little girl! And believe me, I've seen many, Sanjay, but with a cute face and nice body like yours, you'll be the best.
Gemma: Yes, darling, you will! Sanjay is the best in everything he does. Except… - she giggled - in bed.
Deepika: Sanjay, do you want to see your wife sexually satisfied?
Sanjay: Yes, Ms. Deepika. Pleeeeeeease help me to please her, I love her so much eeeeeee - the cries didn't stop.
Deepika: You know there's a condition for you to join our naughty night, let her dress you up with the dress, baby.

With Ms. Deepika's support, Sanjay stays still for a moment and Ms. Gemma uses her hands to put the dress on his head. For a few seconds, he can't see anything, it's all black and blurred with the teardrops that flow freely from his eyes. Then he can see again, the amazing sight of his gorgeous hotwife smiling at him, wearing nothing but a beautiful set of skimpy lingerie showing off her curvy and toned body.

As Ms. Gemma's hands move, working on putting the princess dress on Sanjay's body, her big tits bounce a little bit, making Sanjay turned on. He put his arms up trying to grab her body, his wife dodges his touch but Ms. Deepika grabs his arms in the air and Ms. Gemma seizes the opportunity to make him wear the rest of the cute dress.

It's a pink dress with a tight silky leotard and a tutu skirt that matches the frilly pink panties he is already wearing. Ms. Gemma uses her hands to dress up his arms and then her beloved husband's torso, adjusting the dress here and there with her fingers, caressing his body as she makes the outfit go down. Now it's on his waist, her hands go all around, regulating the length and tightness, making sure it's falling in all the right places.

The skirt with the tutu is a bit hard to fit at first and the two hot babes need to put their hands under the dress to make him wear it nicely. As they do it, Sanjay can feel strong hands on his sissy clitty. Rubbing, touching, stroking. They are taking turns jerking him off and massaging his girly balls as much as forcing him to wear the princess dress.

Deepika: You love when we dress you up, don't you Sanjay?
Sanjay: Yes, Ms. Deepika, it feels good eeeeeeee
Gemma: We could do it every day, sweetie! Imagine you becoming my sweet gay princess forever!
Sanjay: Not every day mommy eeeee pack pack I'm a man - he's quivering and his words fail as he cries, definitely not sounding like a man.
Deepika: You sound like a little girl to me. And you look like a little girl now! So short, with a sissy clitty and girly balls, and now dressed in a cute pink princess dress!
Gemma: I love you, baby! You are the most adorable little girl ever!

- she says uses her hands to put the dress over her husband's head.
Sanjay: eeeee I can't see anything pack - he complains as the dress is placed over his eye, the two hot babe's sexy hands pulling it down using their strong hands.
Deepika: Now you can see yourself wearing a cute little dress, baby - she said as her hands ran down his torso, putting the dress over the bra.
Gemma: Honey, your short body is perfect for this dress! - the blonde woman said as her gorgeous hands made the skirt fall down along her husband's legs.
Deepika: But we are not over yet! - the other woman says as she joins the hotwife, finishing dressing him up in the princess dress.
Sanjay: Pleeeeease stop it eeeeeeeee don't make me do more gay things! pack pack eeeeiiiiiii

Ms. Gemma now takes another gift box and opens it in front of Sanjay and Ms. Deepika. It's a bag of makeup and a wig.

Sanjay: Oh no, not makeup eeeeeee it's too much, mommy, pleeeeease eeeeeee
Gemma: You'll look so cute with makeup on, darling! - she uses her fingers to get facial cream and then she rubs it all over Sanjay's face with her fingertips.
Deepika: Your wife is a great makeup artist, Sanjay, you'll love the results - she uses her hands to keep Sanjay's face in place as Ms. Gemma works all over it.
Gemma: I want to make you the most beautiful little girl ever! - the blonde woman's fingers are touching every inch of Sanjay's face up and down.
Deepika: You are already looking so beautiful! - the ex-girlfriend says, admiring the hot wife's work.
Gemma: Now pout your lips, little girl - her fingers rub lipstick on Sanjay's mouth, making it pink.
Deepika: The best color for a little girl!
Gemma: That's such a puffy little girl's lip - she says as she rubs the tip of her finger all over her husband's lips applying lipstick up and

down.
Gemma: Now close your eyes, honey - she uses her fingers to apply eyeshadow.
Deepika: I hope it's waterproof - she giggles.
Gemma: It is, otherwise it would be ruined, my little girl cries like an overdramatic Bollywood actress! - now she's rubbing her fingers over Sanjay's cheeks, applying blush.
Deepika: Red cheeks like a scared little girl - she notices.
Gemma: Shy and cute like my sissy husband should be - her fingers painting Sanjay's face like a little girl.
Deepika: This is definitely a sissy faggot makeup, so perfect for you, Sanjay!
Gemma: The makeup is done, but the make-over is not yet! - She giggles and takes the wig from the box.
Deepika: The final touch to make you a sweet gay princess, Sanjay! - she says as her hands hold Sanjay's head in a very firm grip.
Gemma: Look at this wig! It's so perfect for my little girl! - She adjusts the wig and then combs it with her fingers.
Deepika: Now your sissy pansy husband really looks like your little girl, wearing a blonde wig.
Gemma: Oh honey, I love how pretty you are with long blonde hair, such a little girl looking like your mommy - her hands massaging Sanjay's scalp, making her relaxed and feel loved.
Deepika: Your sexy fingers disappearing inside your little girl's hairy blonde hair is such a beautiful sight!
Gemma: I'm combing her hair so it looks even prettier, I want my little girl to be the cutest faggot gay princess in the world!
Deepika: I think something is missing, but I'm not sure what.
Gemma: Pigtails! - she says as she uses her hands to grab the hair on one side and Ms. Deepika does the same on the other side, finalizing with the girliest hairstyle.
Deepika: Perfect! Let me help you on this side - her hands pulling the hair and tying it up in a cute way.
Gemma: I love you so much! You are no longer a man, honey. You are my little girl, my Princess Rekha.

Chapter 18 - Not Enough

There she was, completely dressed up as a sweet gay princess. The two hot babes were impressed to look at her for the first time, Princess Rekha was the most adorable little girl. And the faggot sissy was impressed by the looks of the two beautiful women standing in front of him only wearing skimpy lingerie.

Princess Rekha was so turned on by his wife and her college mistress that she couldn't control herself anymore. Her little girl's hands moved in their direction, trying to grope their beautiful round tits. It was met by a gentle slap and giggles.

Gemma: You look so excited, my dear!
Deepika: It's the dress, she's finally turned into a little girl gay princess, your silly faggot sissy husband is out of control.
Gemma: Little girls don't do that, princess - she says as she uses her hands to playfully push Princess Rekha to the bed.
Deepika: Princess Rekha, now that you agree that you'd anything to make your sex life more exciting because you can't please your wife with your micro sissy clitty and girly balls, I have something to announce to you!
Gemma: I can't wait to see Princess Rekha's little girl's face when you say it! - she winked with her sexy eyes.
Deepika: You have been hiding in your little girl gay closet for too long, Princess Rekha, you need a well-hung man to be your wife's new boyfriend and make you more of an obedient little girl for your wife! That's why I'm here, to make sure this will happen with

my expertise - she said in a kind yet serious way.
Princess Rekha: No, Ms. Deepika, pleeeeeeease - she cried like a scared little girl with her dreams of a threesome with the two hot babes shattered - Don't bring another man to my marriage eeeeee pack pack
Gemma: Darling, it's not "another man", it's the only man. You are no longer a man, you are my adorable little girl that I love so much! - she says as she finally sits Princess Rekha down in the bed and touches under her princess dress.
Deepika: You know, Princess Rekha, when I first met you I thought I was in love. I figured that I've finally found my soul mate, a man who's so handsome, strong, intelligent, and successful... After our first and only sexual encounter though, it was so unsatisfying that I began to wonder if there was something wrong with me!
Princess Rekha: No Ms. Deepika eeeee there's nothing wrong with you, just don't find a well-hung boyfriend for Ms. Gemma pleeeeeease pack eeeiiiiii
Gemma: That's so silly, Deepika! You are such an amazing woman, a true goddess! - her sexy hands were touching Princess Rekha's sissy clitty as she said these words, jerking it off.
Deepika: I had to move to another town, change my degree to a different university, it shook my world. In the meantime, I met many men, real men with huge dicks, tall and strong that could please me in bed easily. So different from your premature ejaculator sissy clitty!
Gemma: It's really very small, I only need to use two fingers and even my fingers are longer and thicker than your dicklette honey! - as her hand moved to do a sexy handjob, her magnificent tits bounced up and down, making Princess Rekha get cross-eyed.
Deepika: Our pitiful sexual experience really changed me, I started to contemplate my future if I didn't dare to leave. If I've stayed with such a great man that Sanjay was, despite his shortcomings in bed. I could be happy, but there would always be this side of me that would be incomplete - she grabbed Princess Rekha's girly balls while talking and started to massage them, firmly with her sensual hands.

Gemma: That's exactly how I feel, honey, I love you so much, you are such a wonderful husband but you are a pansy! I could never leave you, I'm loyal to you, my love, and to our wedding vows, that's why Ms. Deepika is here - now her hands started to move quickly, Princess Rekha was breathing heavily in horny anticipation.

Princess Rekha: No Ms. Gemma, don't leave meeeeee eeeeiiiii pack pack

Deepika: I've met many a woman like Ms. Gemma. Trapped in a marriage that yet happy, can never give her the pleasure she deserves because Ms. Gemma is married to a faggot silly sissy, a pansy of a husband with the smallest sissy clitty I've ever seen, it's just not big enough - her grip on Princess Rekha's girly balls got stronger, she was squeezing it with her heavy hands.

Gemma: I'm so happy with you, darling, I'm proud to have such a dedicated and beautiful husband, the best businessman, so rich and prosperous, but everybody has their flaws and yours is in the bed department. I want to bring our marriage to a whole new level, sweetie - she was batting her pretty eyelashes seducing pansy while her hands worked on her sissy clitty.

Deepika: I'm happy you so eagerly accepted to make changes in your relationship! You'll become an obedient little girl for your amazing hotwife Ms. Gemma and her new hunk boyfriend. From now on you'll call her mommy and when you meet her well-hung boyfriend, he will be your daddy and you call him Sir - now Ms. Deepika's hands grabbed the girly balls so hard and pulled them, making Princess Rekha cry out loud.

Princess Rekha: eeeeee don't make me call him daddy eee pleeeease eee pack pack

Gemma: You'll be daddy's little girl, honey! We will teach you how to be a good, cuckold pansy princess. How hot do you think it will be to watch me finally having orgasms on a big cock? - her beautiful hands were going too fast, putting Princess Rekha on the edge of the climax, so she stopped.

The two hot babes let go of Princess Rekha's girly parts at

this moment. They walked a few feet away, Ms. Gemma's curvy body mesmerizing her pansy husband who was sitting down dressed like a sweet gay princess.

The blond wife swayed her wide hips as she walked, the sexy butt cheeks touching each other and swallowing the skimpy panties inside, her ass was so round and perky that it clapped when she moved, the noise happening as her white smooth skin friction from one side of her derriere to the other. She was so tall and looked even taller when Princess Rekha was sitting down.

The brunette mistress wearing black leather boots and black lace lingerie was also an extremely sensual sight to behold. She crossed one of her arms at Ms. Gemma's waist, slightly touching the other woman. Princess Rekha wished it was her touching her hotwife at that moment.

She couldn't take her eyes out of the two statuesque babes, Ms. Deepika was even taller than Ms. Gemma, she felt like a little girl in front of the two towering ladies. Ms. Gemma turned around, wearing white lingerie and also black leather boots, when she faced Princess Rekha, a big smile emerged from her beautiful face and she twirled her blond locks with her thick fingers.

Ms. Deepika also turned, her slender figure hypnotizing Princess Rekha who had her tongue sticking out of her little girl's mouth, almost slobbering like a silly sissy pansy. She knew the two mistresses were too hot for her to handle, but she was so turned on for them anyway.

Gemma: Do you want to touch us, honey? - she said, as she put her arm on her waist, moving her body to the sides, playfully touching her hips on Ms. Deepika's hips.
Deepika: I bet Princess Rekha wants to get her little girl's hands all over us - she said as her own hands on Ms. Gemma's waist went up and touched the side of her big round boobs.
Princess Rekha: Yes mommy eeeee pleeeease, let me have a threesome with two women, not with a man eeee iiiiiii pack pack
Gemma: Is that what you want, sweetie? How would you do that, baby?

Deepika: I think Princess Rekha wants to kiss us - she said as she kissed the blonde woman's neck in a teasing way, making her moan low.

Gemma: humm It feels good, Deepika! Too bad my pansy husband can't make me feel this way because she's too much of a faggot princess! Did you hear her sounding like a little girl just now?

Deepika: I did, sounds like a little girl, acts like a little girl and can't make you moan like a man - she whispered inside Ms. Gemma's ears, but it was audible enough so Princess Rekha could hear.

Gemma: Darling, do you think you can handle two tall sexy women like us?

Princess Rekha: Yes mommy, pleeeease give me a chance to prove eeee iii pack pack

Deepika: Two women in bed with a sissy faggot princess like you, Princess Rekha, means you have the chance to disappoint not only your wife but the two of us at the same time with your sissy clitty and little girl's noises! - she leaned forward a bit to say it and her cleavage was so sexy and exposed, Princess Rekha couldn't take her eyes out of it.

Gemma: And did you hear it now, Deepika? Crying like a silly scared chicken too!

Princess Rekha: Give me sex mommy eeeee I'd do anything pack

Gemma: Honey, I don't think a sissy pansy husband as you should touch us. Little girls with sissy clitties can't give us any pleasure, and your girly balls are empty of fertile cream. Having sex with you is futile!

    The two hot babes started to kiss and make out in front of Princess Rekha, close enough that she could watch in detail, every touch when their sexy hands explored each other's sexy bodies. But it wasn't close enough for her to be the one touching, in a way summing up her whole sexual life: never enough.

Chapter 19 - Too much

Princess Rekha can tell they are getting horny and she's getting frantic, watching her hotwife Ms. Gemma, the blonde tall goddess in white skimpy lingerie doing things to her ex college girlfriend, the sexy tall brunette in black lace bra and panties. The little girl's sissy clitty is hard and throbbing and she craves for her hot wife's sexy hands on it and also the more seasoned and experienced hands of Ms. Deepika.

Princess Rekha: eeee pleeeease mommy, kiss me eeeeiiiii pack pack
Deepika: Poor Princess Rekha, all alone! Gemma, we should give her what she wants otherwise she will cry like a little girl all night!
Gemma: Just like she cries and squeals like a scared Indian bride when we make love! Her face gets contorted and she does a sound like this: eee hai hai iiiii - she mimics her pansy husband's little girl's noises in a loving way.
Deepika: I want to hear it! - the brunette takes her hands out of Ms. Gemma's sexy body and sits down next to Princess Rekha.
Gemma: My little girl sissy of a husband loves when I touch her like this - the hotwife sits down by the other side of the gay princess and puts her strong hands on her thigh, caressing it, lifting up the dress.
Deepika: Does she make these sounds before, during or after getting her sissy clitty wet? - her impeccable hands are also touching Princess Rekha's thighs, going up to meet her sissy clitty.
Gemma: Before intercourse, Princess Rekha begs and cries like a

little girl. She says like "let's have seeeeeeeex eeeee", it's so cute the way she elongates the words as she moans and cries, it's overdramatic just like a Bollywood actress! - she giggles as she impersonates her pansy husband in a caring way.
Deepika: It must be so funny to hear, Princess Rekha is completely in love with you, Gemma! I can tell - her robust hands now pull down the little girl's panties, exposing the tiny cockette and the girly balls.
Gemma: It is! And during love-making, she sounds even more like a silly little girl. Sometimes it goes beyond a pansy sissy, Princess Rekha sounds like a scared chicken or a duck! She goes "pack paaa-aaaaack eeeeeee" - the hotwife grabs Princess Rekha's sissy clitty and jerks it off in a sensual manner.
Deepika: I don't know which one is cuter, it's so on point for Princess Rekha to do these noises - the brunette puts the pansy balls inside the palm of her hands and closes it around it, crushing it gently.
Princess Rekha: eeeeeee pack pack let's have sex already eeeeeee
Deepika: You know that real men don't sound like Princess Rekha, that's why you need someone in your bed that will treat you like you deserve, Gemma. A real man with a big cock, much bigger than this tiny sissy clitty that Princess Rekha has between her little girl's legs - her hands go stronger on Princess Rekha's girly balls, squeezing and twisting it.
Gemma: Princess Rekha was never able to make me cum with her micro cockette or impregnate me because of her girly balls. I really need a huge cock and manly balls full of man cream to make me cum - she says as she strokes Princess Rekha's sissy clitty with her sexy hands nonstop.
Princess Rekha: eeee I promise to try not to cry eeee pack pack pack - she desperately tries, but her mouth is open like a little girl crying and the tears are flowing from her sissy eyes.
Gemma: Oh honey, I'm so happy for your efforts, but you just can't make it work, you are always crying too much like a little girl going eeeeeeeeeee and sounding like a chicken doing pack pack - her hands go so fast now, on the verge to make Princess Rekha's

sissy clitty explode and dribble cum.
Deepika: You are such a pansy little girl, Princess Rekha, you can't keep this kind of promise as much as you want, you'll never be a real man, you are too short and consequently your sissy clitty is small and your balls are so girly! - she giggles and bats her eyes at the little girl.
Gemma: I love you anyway, darling - she winks and smiles at her pansy husband.
Princess Rekha: eee give me seeeeex pleeeease pack - the little girl is so horny, so close to climax that she tries to grope the two hot babes' bodies.

The two women let go of her intimate girly parts and slap her little girl's hands away, making Princess Rekha frustrated, ruining her orgasm. The pansy sissy cries really loud, heartbroken, without her wife's touch, dressed like a silly sissy faggot princess, and sexually frustrated with his tiny sissy clitty hard and untouched.

Deepika: Oh poor little girl, let's give her what she wants, Gemma - she says in a sexy tone as she winks seductively at her partner in crime.
Gemma: Honey, do you really want to touch us? - she wiggles her hips in the most sensual way, her skimpy lingerie showing a lot of her glowing smooth skin.
Princess Rekha: EEee Yes, Ms. Gemma, pleeeease touch my pack pack eeeeiiii sissy clitty eeee pack pack - she finally says, humiliated and defeated, acknowledging the tiny length of her girly parts.
Gemma: We will, darling, come here - the wife smiles and places her hand on her little girl's ears, pulling it up.
Deepika: Stand up, you are such a faggot princess! - she grabs the other ear with her strong hands and pulls it up as well, forcing Princess Rekha on her feet.

Now that Princess Rekha is standing up between the two

beautiful women, they start to hug her, pressing their sexy boobs over her short little girl's body. Their big perky tits are so ripe and squishy, they massage Princess Rekha's torso with them, in the back and in the front.

Ms. Gemma and Ms. Deepika are both so tall compared to Princess Rekha, when they hug the pansy it makes her feel so small, like a little girl. The huge tits all over, so close to her face, but every time she lifts her hands up entertaining the idea of groping these four huge melons, the sissy husband feels slaps on her little girl's hands, forcing her to stay still and just enjoy.

Gemma: I know you want to grab them, darling, but this is not for faggot sissies with tiny dicklettes like you - her eyelashes bat in a seductive way.
Deepika: Sweet gay princess like yourself can never give the pleasure a woman like me and Gemma needs, we need huge cocks and manly balls full of fertile semen, not these pansy girly things you got - her strong able hands pull down Princess Rekha's panties and squeeze her girly balls in her hands.
Princess Rekha: eeee pack pack pleeeeease stop touching me like this eeeee
Gemma: I thought you liked when we hugged you, sweetie - she says as she twists Princess Rekha's ears and pulls it to bring her face closer and kiss her little girl's lips.
Deepika: I'm sure deep down she loves to be treated like the pansy little girl that she has always been, she hid her gay tendencies in her faggot closet for too long! - the brunette goddess starts to twist and pull Princess Rekha's girly balls just like Ms. Gemma is doing to her ears.
Deepika: eeeeeiiiiiiieeeeeeee pack pack No pleeeease, stop it mommy! It's too much eeeeee iiiiiii pack pack iiiiii
Deepika: I think you can handle more, princess! - she grabs the remaining ear with the remaining hand and pulls it in the opposite direction that Gemma is pulling, controlling the short Princess Rekha's body like a cute little girl's puppet.
Gemma: Honey, you want to have a sexy experience with the two

beautiful women for your birthday, so let's dance! - she pulls Princess Rekha's ear even harder now.

The sensation is so strong, Princess Rekha feels like a doll, pulled and pinches around without any control. When she struggles and tries to get away, Ms. Gemma's strong hands slap her pansy husband in the face. It was the first time anyone has ever slapped Princess Rekha, let alone her own hot wife! The physical sensation was intense because the slap was hard, and where her thick fingers became red, a warm and sharp sensation irradiating all over her face.

The ears being pulled also brought this kind of sensation, warm and sore, and it encountered the painful wave coming from her cheeks. Her skin was hurting, but what she felt even harder was the humiliation of being beaten by two hot women that tricked her to think she was going to have sex, and verbally degraded her because of her diminutive sexual organ and are now proving she's completely useless in bed by acting like she's nothing but a silly little girl.

Princess Rekha started to cry with real tears for the first time in front of her wife or anyone. The physical and psychological pain was just too much.

Chapter 20 - Someone New

Gemma: Oh honey, you look so cute when you cry - she uses her hands to make Princess Rekha lay her little girl's head on her boobs, consoling pansy in a caring way.
Deepika: I know someone that would love to see this faggot sissy acting like an adorable little girl! - she says excitedly as her hands move between the Princess legs.
Princess Rekha: Who, Ms. Deepika? - the little girl whimpers with tears trickling down her face.
Deepika: I'm going to introduce Gemma to her new potential boyfriend. A white man, because white men are superior to Asian men, especially in the bed department - the mistress grabs Princess Rekha's tiny clitty and rubs it.
Princess Rekha: No pleeeeeease, don't do it Ms. Deepika eeeeee - the little girl cries and sniffles.
Deepika: Do you want me to stop? - she takes her hands out of the sissy clitty.
Princess Rekha: Noooo eeeeeee pack pack Don't stop eeeeee
Gemma: You are such a silly little girl, darling! Listen to yourself, you don't even know what you want, that's why you need women like me and Ms. Deepika to tell you what to do and how to live your life, for your own sake, sweetie - she smiles with her sexy lips.
Deepika: And we decided to find a well-hung man to be your wife's new boyfriend and make you more of an obedient little girl! - the brunette lady winks.
Gemma: Yes, baby, I'm so excited! You'll even call him daddy as we teach you to be a good, cuckold pansy princess that I love so much!

- the blonde winks back, her eyelashes so sensual, making Princess Rekha cross-eyed with so much beauty.
Princess Rekha: No mommy, pleeeease, don't make me call him daddy eeeeeee
Deepika: You'll love to see your new daddy's huge cock - the woman uses her hands again on the sissy clitty and then compares it to her own pinky finger and giggles.
Gemma: How big is he, Deepika?
Deepika: He has a massive white cock with huge balls full of fertile man cream - she shows with her hands the size of about 10 inches.
Gemma: Wow I'm impressed! I'm not sure if I can handle that much! - the wife sounds genuinely worried for a second.
Deepika: Oh my dear, you'll love to learn how to handle it! In fact, you are tall and strong, your body was made to have sex with tall white men with big cocks, and not with short Indian men with micro cockettes and girly balls.
Gemma: But I love my short pansy husband despite his dicklette.
Deepika: I know you do, but it's not about love, it's science. There's a reason your pansy gay husband could never satisfy you sexually and never get you pregnant, your own body rejects it because Princess Rekha is nothing but a little girl.
Gemma: That's true, it never felt natural for me, although I've always been loyal to Princess Rekha. I'm so happy you are in our lives now, Deepika! You'll bring someone new to save my marriage.
Deepika: His name is Frank. But for you, Princess Rekha, his name is daddy!
Princess Rekha: Nooo don't make me call him daddy, don't bring another man to our marriage eeee pack pack eeeeeee - the snivel intensifies.
Gemma: Honey, you'll have to accept it. Do you want to have sex again? - she asks while masturbating her pansy husband's sissy clitty with her sexy strong hands.
Princess Rekha: Yes eeeee pleeeease Ms. Gemma, give me sex eeee pleeeease eee pack pack
Deepika: You'll have sex again, Princess Rekha, I promise you. After we completely feminize you, take you out of your pansy gay

closet and turn you into the little girl that you were born to be!

Princess Rekha: pack pack eeeee just give me sex now pleeeeease eeee

Gemma: I can't wait to meet my new boyfriend, his cock is so much bigger than your sissy clitty, honey! - her sexy hands never stop jerking off Princess Rekha's dicklette.

Deepika: You'll never want to touch this little thing again, I promise you - she giggles as she rubs the girly balls with her hands.

Gemma: I bet these pansy balls are so full, can you feel it, Deepika?

Deepika: Barely! Pansy balls hardly produce enough sissy cream, that's why they are so small and girly. You'll be impressed by your new hunk boyfriend's big balls. By the way, Big Balls is what Frank is called in some circles. They are huge!

Princess Rekha: eeeee stop talking about big balls eeeee pleeeease release my blue girly balls - the little girl is panting, almost reaching climax.

Deepika: Huge big balls full of man cream, we will give you a taste, Princess Rekha. Your little gay mouth will love to experience a big cock and drink man cream like the faggot cuckold that you are - she says while giving Princess Rekha a hot handjob with her sexy experienced big and strong hands.

Princess Rekha: eeeee pleeeease Ms. Gemma, don't let Ms. Deepika do it to me eeeee just give me sex now eeee - the faggot princess is desperate and falls down to her knees, completely broken.

Gemma: Sweetie, you know you can't bring any of us to orgasm, by not giving you sex I'm saving you from disappointing not only me, your loving wife, but also avoiding you to embarass yourself with your ex-girlfriend too - she explains helping Ms. Deepika to wank the sissy clitty fast and hard with her perfectly manicured hands.

Princess Rekha: eeeeee just let me finish now pleeeease eeee I'm having blue balls, save me mommy eeeee

Gemma: But you need to stand up, honey, you are so short that when you are on your knees we can barely see you! - the two hot babes take their hands out of the sissy clitty and girly balls, grab the little girl's ears and pull them up to make her stand.

Gemma: Good girl! I love to see you dressed like the faggot princess

that you hid from me, you are mommy's little girl now, darling.
Deepika: And you'll love to have a daddy, a manly figure in the house, treating you like the little girl that you are.
Princess Rekha: Pleeease stop the boyfriend talk now eeeeee - she tries to run away from the two hot babes sobbing, so weakly.
Gemma: Don't be afraid, sweetheart, you are acting like a scared Indian bride crying so loud overdramatically, I bet you learned this watching Bollywood actresses! - the tall blonde uses her big strong arms to stop Princess Rekha from running away, giving her a headlock.
Princess Rekha: eeee mommy let me go eeeeeee don't force me to meet my new daddy eeeee - she protests and cries as she feels her wife's strong muscled arms around her little girl's head.
Deepika: It will be easier if you don't struggle, Princess Rekha. Ms. Gemma will dress you up with her own hands every day, you'll be spoiled and pampered like the little girl that you are, sleeping in a pink room wearing pink frilly panties and watching gay porn all day! - the brunette says, full of joy.
Gemma: Deepika, is it true that before being a successful businessman Frank also starred in porn? - her arms still around Princess Rekha's little girl's head, forcing her to hear every detail.
Deepika: It's true! He is so handsome, with a ripped muscled body, so tall and his cock is so big that he was paid a little fortune to perform naked. Maybe Princess Rekha has seen Frank before in one of her gay magazines!
Princess Rekha: eeeee don't make me look at naked men eeee pack pack don't make me gay pleeeease eeeee
Deepika: Too late, princess! Your pansy gay closet is wide open and you can't hide there anymore!
Gemma: When are we meeting him, Deepika?
Deepika: Maybe I should call Frank right now so you and Princess Rekha can meet your new well-hung boyfriend tonight!
Gemma: Oh my god, I can't wait for it! Do it! - the headlock becomes even stronger now, so Princess Rekha can't cry out loud, her groans are muffled.
Gemma: We are ready to add someone new to our marriage, aren't

we honey? - she winks and bats her sensual eyelashes and smiles at her pansy husband locked between her beautiful muscled arms, who can't run away or reply, all Princess Rekha can do at this moment is quietly acquiesce as the last drops of tears are squeezed out of her little girl's eyes.

Chapter 21 - Frank "Big Balls" James

Rekha couldn't talk while completely subdued in her wife's headlock; Ms. Gemma had special cops training and she can fight like a superheroine, using her strong hands with ability and perfection. Her short little girl pansy of a husband is an easy prey facing the statuesque toned sexy blonde.

The sissy whimpering and whining were inaudible but the little girl could hear Ms. Deepika talking to someone. His voice was so strong and manly that the sound went beyond the phone making pansy shiver when the man said he was in the neighborhood and would arrive in just a few minutes.

During the brief wait, the two hot babes put their clothes back on, covering the skimpy lingerie with sexy tight dresses. The little girl remained clothed in her gay princess dress, to her shame.

And he did. The doorbell rang, Ms. Deepika went to the front door to open it while Ms. Gemma pulled Princess Rekha to the master bedroom still using the headlock, moving her around not like a man, but as if her sissy husband were a little girl puppet doll, ready to obey.

Princess Rekha could hear the door creaking open, then Ms. Deepika greeted and invited someone in, the steps coming closer and closer until they entered the master bedroom. What used to be the couple's love nest, the safe haven where Sanjay, the businessman, and loving husband, could rest after a long hard day of work with his amazing wife was now the torment of Princess Rekha, the silly sissy dressed like a little girl and about to witness her hotwife meeting her new hunk boyfriend, someone that could provide everything he couldn't: a satisfying sexual life, body shaking orgasms, and the fulfillment of Ms. Gemma's long-standing dream of having a baby.

There he was. Frank "Big Balls" James in flesh and blood. Princess Rekha felt extremely self-conscious looking at the man in front of him. He was so tall, even Ms. Gemma and Ms. Deepika had to look up to talk to him, something that Princess Rekha never had happened to her. She could only imagine the power that a real man that tall could have on women.

Frank was wearing a nice tailored suit that covered his big ripped muscles. White skin, a head full of light blondish hair and green piercing eyes. An eye candy to the ladies and the impression he made on the two hot babes was obvious, they were full smiles, playing with their hair and flirting as soon as he entered the room. Princess Rekha never experienced anything like this, being a short asian pansy with a little girl's voice with a lisp.

Deepika: Gemma, this is Frank. Frank, this is Gemma - she said, introducing the two white blondes to each other.
Gemma: Hi! - she said smiling with her sexy lips while still holding down Princess Rekha in an armlock while she trembles like a scared chicken.
Frank: Hello! Nice to see you today, Deepika, thank you for introducing me to your beautiful friend Gemma! Gemma, you look lovely today, even prettier than Deepika told me.
Gemma: You are too kind! Are you ready to meet my faggot pansy husband, Princess Rekha?
Deepika: You have to greet him correctly, princess, like the adorable little girl that you are.
Gemma: Yes, honey, let me teach you how to do it - the headlock is still on, very tight because pansy is shaking and sobbing uncontrollably, her free hand comes from behind and grabs her pansy balls.

Deepika: Time for the curtesy! - she giggles in awe.
Gemma: Darling, you'll call him Sir - Princess Rekha's arm is tied behind her sissy back, Ms. Gemma pulls her balls down forcing her to make a curtsey.
Princess Rekha: eeeeeee Nice to meeeeeet you, Sir! pack pack pack eeeeeeee
Gemma: You are such a good little girl, you make me proud, sweetie! I love you so much!
Frank: I can see you gorgeous ladies really know how to train a little girl. I already love you, Gemma, and I want you to have my baby.
Gemma: This is a dream I have had for such a long time! I'm falling in love with you and am ready to have your baby!
Frank: Are you, gorgeous? - he asks in his deep sexy voice.
Gemma: For years I thought I loved my pansy husband, but the more I got to know my little girl, the more I knew I needed a real man to love me back.
Frank: What do you mean, gorgeous?
Gemma: What I feel for my sissy faggot husband is something different. I do love her like a little girl, my sweet gay princess, but it's different from the love of a husband and wife - she confessed.
Frank: I'm ready to dedicate my love for you, Ms. Gemma. The love of a man.
Gemma: I have fallen out of love with my sissy husband. And now I love you, Frank, as a woman.
Frank: I love you, Ms. Gemma, I love you so much. I want to be your man, I want to make you my woman. I love you more than a little girl ever could.
Gemma: I know, Frank. And now I know that I love you the way I could never love my little girl, she's just a little girl, a sissy faggot pansy, and I need the love of a real man. I want you to be the man of the house, I want to make you a real woman and give me your babies. I've fallen in love with you, Frank.

Princess Rekha can't believe what she's hearing. After so many years of marriage, being a loyal and devoted husband, her hotwife Gemma is declaring her love to another man in front of her and making plans to have his baby!

The realization that to make a baby sex is needed strikes Princess Rekha like lightning. They are planning on making love, right there in the master bedroom, perhaps even that very night! She has become an obedient cuckold pansy of a husband, making curtsies and calling her hot wife's well-hung boyfriend "Sir".

Princess Rekha is blushing in shame because she might be crying and sobbing but deep down there's a part of her that is excited. She couldn't stop staring at Frank's "Big Balls" crotch. There's a big package there and she wonders if these are the famous Big Balls or something else...

Chapter 22 - Princess Meets Frank

Ms. Deepika is, among other things, a professional matchmaker. She gets pleasure from finding a well-hung boyfriend for neglected wives that suffer from a lack of sexual compatibility with their pansy husbands with tiny cockettes. When she met Ms. Gemma, she instantly knew who she would pair her with. Ms. Gemma and Sanjay - now Princess Rekha - were a special couple and for that, it needed to be perfect, she saved Frank "Big Balls" James for the best because his lovemaking skills were out of this world, and Ms. Gemma needed that!

Deepika: I'm so happy you came to meet us so fast, Frank! Because we have a situation here that only you can fix.
Gemma: I really think he is the one, Deepika! - she plays with her blond locks in a flirting way.
Deepika: He is! I could tell you immediately fell in love with this fine hunk man, love at first sight!
Gemma: I love my husband, but there are certain things that he just can't give to me. It's been so many years, I tried, I was patient and understanding, yet his anatomy will never change. I am married to a shorty pansy with a sissy clitty that moans like a little girl.
Deepika: Like this? - she says as she grabs the pansy balls with her strong hands and squeezes them.
Princess Rekha: eeeeeeee pack pack my little girly balls are blue, Ms. Deepika eeeeee
Gemma: Exactly like this! - she giggles, batting her eyes.

Deepika: You see Frank, Gemma is married to a real little girl who could never satisfy her in bed - the ballbusting continues, the pansy balls now inside her big hand that is clenched around as a fist.
Princess Rekha: eeee i'm not a little girl eee pack pack I'm a man! eeiiiiiiii
Gemma: Oh honey, you don't need to pretend just because Frank is here, we all know you are a pansy gay princess! - she smiles and winks at her husband in a loving way.
Deepika: That's why we dress you like a little girl, Princess Rekha. You need to be fully feminized to watch your wife with her new lover and see all the things you could never do with your tiny cockette.
Gemma: It's really super small, Frank. I'm even a little shy to confess that I could never feel anything with Princess Rekha while having sex, it's not even a cockette, it's a sissy clitty! - she says as she grabs the little girl's dicklette in her hands and compares it to her little finger, which is bigger and thicker than the sissy clitty.
Deepika: It's the smallest I've ever seen, and I've seen many! You'll see how different it will be with Frank and his massive cock and big balls full of fertile man cream.
Princess Rekha: Pleeeeease eeeee don't have sex with other men, mommy, eeeeeee pack eeeeee

By hearing again the whining and whimpers from the little girl, Ms. Deepika used her free hand to smack Princess Rekha's faggot face with a slap. The thick fingers hit across her cheek and the exact location where it landed made the pansy feel a sting. The sensation irradiated through the whole face and made the sissy husband burst into tears.

Princess Rekha was so ashamed to be beaten up by a woman, in front of her wife and her potential new boyfriend. Worst of all, the sissy princess could notice that somehow the bulge inside Frank's pants got bigger. Apparently, he was getting turned on by the ordeal she was going through and now the little girl was sure about what she suspected the whole time: Frank had big balls and an even bigger white cock!

Gemma: I know you want what's best for me, darling, and I want what's best for you! I love you, Princess Rekha, and Frank is here to be your daddy! You'll be dressed up every day like daddy's little girl, prancing around like the pansy that you are, and watch this fine man fill in where you have been lacking.
Princess Rekha: eeeee noooo eeeeee pack pack I don't want that eeeee
Deepika: Princesses doesn't talk like that, be a good little girl for your mommy! - she says as her hands strike once again on the little girl's face.
Princess Rekha: eeeeiiiii pack pack eeeeee Stop pleeeeease eeeeee
Gemma: Baby, you know you are perfect in every department, you are handsome, with a beautifully strong body, so smart and successful, but there's an exception, darling. There's one very important department, you are so small... your stature and your cockette! And you just don't know how to use it properly. You are no good in bed, honey!
Princess Rekha: You can't do this to meeeee eeeee pack pack eeeeee - her little girl's mouth is shivering and her face is contorted as she cries.
Gemma: It's way too small for any woman to ever feel pleased with this little thing, sweetie. And it's like you know it, your body knows it's useless because you always cum so quickly, you are so fast on the trigger, honey - she grabs Princess Rekha's ears and pulls them to keep her in place.
Deepika: It's the most important department in a marriage, that's why a hot wife like you Gemma needs a well-hung boyfriend like Frank, to step up where Princess Rekha can't - she uses both of her sexy strong hands to slap Princess Rekha's face, taking turns between busting her pansy balls and hitting her face.
Gemma: I do need someone to indulge my urges, darling. You are nothing but a little girl with a sissy clitty and girly balls, there's nothing down there that you can give to me, sweetheart - now she twists the little girl's ears and it starts to get red.

Deepika: Frank, I don't think you have ever seen such an effeminate pansy like Princess Rekha before. Can you hear how she cries like a little girl? - the brunette goddess intensifies the slaps.

Princess Rekha: eeeee pleeeeease stop it, Ms. Deepika eeeeee pack pack eeeeeiiii - she has yet another crying fit, her face covered in tears, her jaw shivering.

Gemma: It's cute that she makes the same noises when she cries when she cums! Like a little girl and sometimes even sounding like a scared chicken.

Princess Rekha: pack pack eeee pack pack I'm not a chicken! eeee pack pack pack - while denying, the little girl sounded even more like a chicken.

Deepika: Just like this! Squealing like a silly scared chicken!

Chapter 23 - XOXO

The situation was totally in Ms. Deepika's control. She was an experienced mistress in her game, manipulating everyone with excellent timing. She knew that Ms. Gemma would fall in love with Frank as soon as she saw him, she also knew that talking about Princess Rekha's faults would make the little girl more susceptible to obey. Lastly, she had the knowledge that well-hung hunks like Frank would get turned on by watching pansy getting beaten up. They were all in her hands and it was time for things to get serious!

Ms. Deepika notices that the little girl is about to break down on her knees crying again, interfering with the romance between the wife and her new potential boyfriend. So the brunette mistress put Princess Rekha into a headlock, restraining her. She's shaking, crying, but still and watching everything with attention.

As the sissy is fully controlled and subdued by the other woman, Ms. Gemma feels more comfortable approaching Frank. She couldn't take her eyes off the tall muscled man since he entered the room.

Gemma: Welcome to my house, Frank! I didn't greet you properly yet - she says as she comes closer to the man and hugs and kisses his cheek.
Frank: Thank you, gorgeous - his strong arms come around the blonde woman's body, embracing her.
Gemma: What do you think of my outfit, Frank? I wore it special

for you - she said, twirling, making his sexy hands touch her back and front, getting excited by his touch.

Ms. Gemma changed her outfit prior to Frank's arrival, putting on a tight red dress that showed her curvy body in a spectacular way. The dress had a big cleavage that left the upper part of her magnificent breasts on display, and a slit on the lower part revealing her toned legs all the way up to the thighs.
She was wearing high heels shoes that made her even taller than before, towering in front of the short little girl, yet she was no match to the hunk man who was many inches taller than her.
When they hug, Princess Rekha can see his hands going to Ms.

Frank: I love what you are wearing, you are so sexy, I'm completely in love with you - he said as his hands went over her body, hugging and touching every inch.
Gemma: I'm so in love with you! Welcome to my house, my love!

Gemma's back is touched up and down, bringing a horny shiver to the woman's body. The sissy husband wanted to cry when he noticed that just the touch of the well hung white man's hands on her wife's body had a more intense result than when they used to make love.
Then his hands go to her legs and pull her dress a bit up, making the blonde woman blush. Frank doesn't stop and teases her with his big thick fingers, making sure to make her body shiver in horniness as he touches her lustfully.

Frank: Thank you, Gemma. This is a beautiful house and you are an even more beautiful lady - he kisses her mouth, his meaty lips touching her delicate mouth.
Gemma: You are so sweet! Your presence here makes it even more beautiful. I can't stop looking at your beautiful tall body and wondering what you have under these clothes! - the hotwife kisses the tall man back.

There was only one way to know! Ms. Gemma's impeccable hands dab the man's shoulders, they were so broad! She slowly took his jacket off, revealing his muscled chest.

Gemma: Wow you are very committed to the gym, Frank! - she remarked as she started to open the buttons of his shirt. One by one, her thick long fingers touched his body under the shirt and gradually revealed his naked white skin.
Gemma: I want to touch your muscles with my hands, with my lips, with all my body - she said as she rubbed and kissed his hot body.
Gemma: You look even better without this! It's just so weird to me that I have to look up to your face when I do this, because you are so tall! Yet it feels natural, like it's supposed to be. My pansy faggot husband, Princess Rekha, is such a little girl, so short, even her clothes are little girl's sized! However, look at your shirt... It's so big, you are so much big than my gay princess husband! I wonder what other big things you have - she giggles as she finishes undressing Frank's torso, leaving him shirtless. Now her hands go between his legs.
Gemma: Well, well, what we have here! I can't believe it's so massive and so hard! So different from my silly sissy husband, Princess Rekha has a very small dicklette - she rubs his enormous cock over the clothes and smiles happily.
Gemma: I can't wait to see it! - her perfect hands open Frank's pants and unzip them, pulling them down. His underwear was tight and full making the man look like an underwear model.
Gemma: Oh my god, it's throbbing! - she puts her robust hands inside the boxer and gets ahold of a big cock for the first time in her life.
Gemma: I'm speechless! It's way too big, Princess Rekha's sissy clitty is so tiny and her girly balls are also so cute and delicate. I'm not used to being around a real man like you, Frank! Especially when it comes to your manly parts! - she's blushing but she never stops touching.

Gemma: I want it badly - Ms. Gemma undresses the white hunk man completely, leaving him in the nude. She takes a few steps back just to admire the man with perfect measurements, looking like a pornographically enhanced Greek statue.
Gemma: Touching your humongous cock makes me feel alive again! - she needed her two hands to hold his huge cock.
Gemma: You are so different from my pansy husband, Frank! He is such a little girl in height and cockette size compared to a big, sexy, powerful hunk like yo... - the last word was only spoken in half because her sensual lips met the man's mouth and they kissed passionately.

His hands were all over Ms. Gemma's body and Princess Rekha could see it all. They were hugging, while her wife jerked off Frank's big cock, his hands were touching her back and then squeezing her butt. Their lips were locked, the two were kissing deeply with tongues. Even a few muffled moans could be heard during their makeout session.

Frank's big thick fingers made sure to touch every inch of the hot blonde's wife and even her face, making her sigh like a woman in love. She was whispering vows of love between her moans.

Frank: I love you so much, Gemma - their hot bodies so close as they hug and kiss.
Gemma: I love you, Frank! So much more than I ever loved my pansy husband, you are the man that owns my heart now - she grinds her hips against his body, the lust taking over her body and feelings.

Princess Rekha was crying like a little girl, trembling in despair on Ms. Deepika's headlock because her beloved wife is trembling with pleasure in Frank's arms.

Chapter 24 - All The Things that Mouths Can Do!

Frank's hands are wandering all over Ms. Gemma's body while they kiss and hug, running all the way up her legs and skilfully pulling her dress up. Princess Rekha is staring, looking at Ms. Gemma's luscious body, and wishing it was her touching the hotwife instead.

Eventually, the dress goes to her waist, putting her wide hips on display with a pair of sexy skimpy white panties. Pansy had seen the lingerie already but the sight of her wife's underwear made her lust come in full, she could feel her sissy clitty getting hard but the only genital Ms. Gemma seemed interested was in Frank's huge cock, which measured three times bigger than Princess Rekha's sissy clitty.

Ms. Gemma squeals in heavenly delight and anticipation when she touches Frank's massive cock, his hands go up her torso drawing her dress all the way up until it's off her gorgeous body. Frank wasted no time and masterfully unclipped her bra, freeing her splendid breasts. They are full and ripe like a delicious fruit and Frank gropes them with both hands, kissing her entire bosom with his sexy lips until reaching her nipples.

Deepika: Can you see how hard her nipples are? It means she's horny and ready for the stud. I bet her panties are also so wet! - the brunette whispered in Princess Rekha's ears, teasing and taunting her.

The woman's nipples were hard and ready to be gorged by his massive tongue, licking in circles, making her moan, and then putting his sensual mouth over them and sucking, feasting on her feminine figure. Frank was taking turns with her boobs, sucking one and playing with the other with his hands, Ms. Gemma was rubbing her thighs together, she was so horny and ready to take him inside.

Deepika: She can barely control herself! I bet you've never seen your hotwife acting like this before! Pansy sissies like you don't have this kind of power over women like well-hung alpha males have - the armlock was still tight and all Princess Rekha could do was cry.

The man starts to kiss the rest of her body on the way down until reaching her panties, his big hands slowly take them down, revealing Ms. Gemma's smooth pubic mound. Her pussy lips glistening with juices welcome his thick finger as he rubs her clit and makes the hotwife moan out loud. It's just as loud as Princess Rekha's cries as she squeaks like a scared little girl in a horror movie, although Frank was ready to perform another kind of movie genre.

Gemma: This is so big, Frank, at least three times bigger than my husband's sissy clitty! I need to taste you, you look delicious - she says as she lays Frank down on the bed, kisses his lips, his neck, and goes down to his body with kisses.
Gemma: You are such a fantastic alpha hunk of a stud! The complete opposite to my little girl of a husband, always so silly, a gay pansy that could never make me feel this good! - she reaches his large penis and big balls.
Gemma: Your nickname was not a joke, your balls are so manly, they are hefty! So heavy and huge, I'm impressed - she sucks on his balls, barely able to put even one of them inside her mouth.
Gemma: My pansy husband's balls are really girly and small, I

never imagined all the ecstasy I missed out on being with a real man - her tongue goes up to the base of his big cock and she licks all the way to the top, flicking her sexy tongue at the slit and tasting his precum.

Gemma: You are so delicious! - she puts the head of his massive cock inside her mouth and starts to suck him.

Ms. Gemma's mouth was not used to such big things and in the beginning, she had a difficult time giving a blowjob to Frank. She licked and kissed the tip, but when it was time to put the shaft in her mouth she gagged. Princess Rekha could hear her choking noises as she gurgled down, inch by inch. It was impossible to take the whole thing because Frank's cock was humongous, but little by little Ms. Gemma showed to be a fast learner. The lust and desire that man produced in her made the hotwife deepthroat as deep as humanly possible, taking almost the entire member inside her mouth.

Deepika: I bet she never sucked you like this! Your tiny sissy clitty is not worth the trouble, it's way too small. Only big cocks get them an appetite! - she giggled, knowing the words hurt like the slaps she gave before.

Princess Rekha couldn't believe what she was watching, her wife sucking dick like a pro, with so much gusto like she never did with her. To be honest, Ms. Gemma always giggled when Princess Rekha suggested a blowjob and only gave a few licks. The sad fact was that it was enough for her to explode all over Ms. Gemma's sexy lips and she couldn't believe how long Frank was able to hold himself from cumming.

The oral sex lasted about 20 minutes, it was so intense, with so much sucking and slurping until finally he cums inside her mouth and she swallowed every drop of it with a big sly smile on her face. The hotwife never swallowed her pansy husband's cum before and it made the sissy cry again.

Deepika: Ms. Gemma just received a treat for her effort. With you she doesn't even need to try, your premature ejaculation takes all the fun out of it!

After the blowjob, they hugged and kissed for a long time, laying in bed together. Frank got on top of the blonde goddess and started to kiss her body, it was his turn. He kissed her neck, stopped at her breasts, and sucked each one of her nipples without hurry, listening to her moans and watching her body squirming in pleasure.

Then he went down, kissing her flat tummy and then her inner thighs, teasing her, making her open her legs wide. Princess Rekha could see her perfect pussy so wet and engorged, ready to be penetrated as he had never seen before. They always had to use artificial lube to have sex because the hotwife never got wet for her.

Frank took his time to taste her juices, rejoicing at every horny groan she made due to the touch of his thick tongue in her intimate parts. The stud was so skilled, he was sipping on her lubrication juices with his big sexy lips and massive tongue, reaching parts that had never been touched before.

Deepika: Even Frank's tongue is bigger than your sissy clitty, no wonder Ms. Gemma is enjoying it so much! She will never have sex with you again.

Ms. Deepika's words echoed inside Princess Rekha's sissy brain along with Ms. Gemma's moans at Frank's superior sexual skills. She knew it was true and the only thing that could surpass these sounds was the noise of her own cries. The desperate cry of a little girl.

Chapter 25 - Love, Sex, Fuck

Ms. Gemma's thighs are around Frank's head, she's moving her hips up and down trying to get more and more of his tongue inside of her. Princess Rekha watches in dread because she knows her sissy clitty is smaller than the hot stud's long tongue and it still seems to be not enough for the hot wife. Her body needs a big cock, she wants more than a tongue.

Deepika: His is warming her up with his tongue, Princess Rekha. You probably don't know what it is because your tiny cockette is almost invisible, but to have sex with a big cock, a woman needs to be very turned on. Seems like Gemma is ready to be owned! - the brunette mistress sounded aroused.

Frank's mouth was busy, his sexy lips touching Ms. Gemma's perfect pussy lips in the most erotic type of kiss, but his green eyes were staring at her face, understanding how she reacts to his every move. Her bright eyes are winking at him and her sensual mouth is asking for more between horny moans. When she's on the edge of an orgasm, he stops.

Deepika: You are about to witness something magical and unique. It's like Gemma is a virgin about to be deflowered, your wife will be penetrated by a big cock for the first time, it will touch parts that your sissy clitty was never able to, and it will be inside of her much longer than you could ever do!

The tall sexy blonde is breathing heavily, her legs are open inviting the hot stud in her entrails. He positioned himself, aiming his long fat throbbing white cock at the entrance of her perfect wet pussy. Ms. Gemma holds Frank's hands as he slowly conquers every inch inside of her with his powerful dick. Slowly at first, stopping every few seconds and allowing her to accommodate his enormous size.

    She takes it all with great delight, a lustful joy that only the best sex can entail, something she never experienced with her faggot pansy of a husband. Princess Rekha knew it, she had never seen her hot wife like this before.

Deepika: She's having the time of her life, Princess Rekha! He is on top of her, giving her a big cock in a position you could never do because your dicklette is so tiny she always needed to be on top!

    Princess Rekha can't take her eyes out of her beautiful tall white wife taking a huge white cock, making her a cuckold sissy husband. The first minutes were slow and romantic, the lovemaking lasted a lot longer than Princess Rekha ever did while having sex. When Ms. Gemma was ready, the pace changed. Now they were fucking! Frank was ramming his huge cock inside Ms. Gemma's tight horny pussy, her big boobs bouncing with the movement and the room was filled with the sexiest feminine sexy moans ever heard.

Deepika: I know she never moaned like this with your sissy clitty, because this only can happen with a real man, never with a little girl!

    They were going so hard, Princess Rekha was sure that Frank was about to cum and she panicked at this thought. They were not using condoms and Ms. Gemma was a very fertile woman. The idea of her loving wife carrying the baby of another man, made Princess Rekha try to get away from Ms. Deepika's arms and try to stop it, but her ex-girlfriend was so much taller and stronger than her, she easily controlled the little girl's impulse by fastening the headlock even harder.

To Princess Rekha's amusement, Frank didn't finish inside his hot wife. At least not now, the hot stud had so much control of his body and his huge cock that he only ejaculated at his own demand and it was not time yet.

Ms. Gemma turned over and got on all fours, Princess Rekha could watch her wife's big juicy ass so pretty, her legs opened just enough so both her tantalizing holes could be seen pulsating with desire. Frank positioned himself right behind Ms. Gemma and resumed the hard fuck, sticking his huge cock as deep as he could inside the hot blonde. Frank's big balls were slapping against Ms. Gemma's clit, driving her even hornier and making slapping noises.

Deepika: You could never do this position, Princess Rekha, it's the one that requires the longest dick, with a sissy clitty like yours is impossible. Your girly balls never made this kind of noise, am I right? - she winks and giggles at the little girl that whimpers silently knowing Ms. Deepika is always right.

The sight is so hot to behold, Princess Rekha would do anything to be part of it. Frank's balls are so big that it's possible to watch when they vibrate and flutter, his load is ready, the hot stud is about to fill Ms. Gemma with man cream.

Quickly, Frank pulls the woman's leg, making her lay on the side. He's still on top, holding her leg up and able to watch her whole body as he pumps every drop of his fertile semen inside Ms. Gemma's perfect pussy. The well-hung moan so loud, in such a heavy, manly, and proud way when he cums that Princess Rekha almost made susu in her panties hearing to his virile groan.

Deepika: That's hot a real man moan, Princess Rekha. Not like this - she squeezes the princess girly balls by surprise making her squeal like a chicken.

Frank withdrew from Ms. Gemma's pussy but his huge cock was still ejaculating and two more thick streams landed all over her big beautiful tits. His job was done but Princess Rekha's part was yet to come.

Deepika: Now it's your turn, little girl! Open your mouth! - she forces the sissy to go closer to her wife, her head still in the armlock.
Gemma: Honey, you waited so much, now it's time for you to feast! - she says happily, winking at her pansy husband and using her hands to force the princess's mouth wide open - her sexy hands hold Princess Rekha in place.
Princess Rekha: eeeee nooo I don't want leftovers eeee pack pack
Deepika: Lick it like the good little girl that you are! - the brunette's strong hands rub the faggot ballerina's mouth all over Ms. Gemma's pussy, taking advantage that to the fact that she opened the mouth to speak, forcing her to eat it.
Gemma: I know you'll love man cream, darling - she flexes her pussy muscles, her perfect pussy lips open up as she pushes the whole load out for Princess Rekha to drink it.
Princess Rekha: eeee slurp slurp eeeeeee no more man cream eeeee pack slurp - she swallows every drop.
Deepika: We are not over, there's more up in there - she points to Ms. Gemma's magnificent breasts covered in white man cream.
Gemma: Come here, sweetie, I know you love to lay your head on mommy's boobs when you are crying - she forces Princess Rekha's head on her big tits, consoling her by caressing her hair as she cries and sucks on her big tits, licking the remaining of Frank's huge load of man cream.
Deepika: You are such an adorable little girl! Good job!
Gemma: You did it so well, honey, you even have a little girl's white mustache of man cream now! - she giggles as she cleans her little girl's with her thick long fingers.

Chapter 26 - The Pink Room

Gemma: Baby, it's official now. I have a new boyfriend, darling. He will be the man of the house now, he is going to take your place in the bedroom because you are nothing but a little girl - she smiles batting her sexy eyes.
Deepika: You did so great, Gemma!
Gemma: The master bedroom is no longer your place, sweetheart. Come here, I'll show you your new bedroom. This is yet another surprise I've made for our special day! - the two hot babes use their hands to grab Princess Rekha's ear and pull them to move her around the house.
Princess Rekha: Eeeee pack pack let me sleep in the master bedroom eeeeee I want to be with mommy! pack eeeeiiiii - she cries and resists, but the two goddesses are much taller and stronger than pansy and her objection is futile.
Deepika: You'll love your new little girl's pink room!

Princess Rekha is brought to what they had planned to be the nanny's bedroom, but she was never able to make Ms. Gemma's pregnant so the room remained useless until then. It was completely remodeled, painted in pink all over with a nice cute princess bed in the middle.

There was a pink closet full of girly gay outfits, from dresses to underwear, shoes, wigs and makeup! But what caught everyone's attention was the posters of naked men all over the room, centerfold from the playgirl magazines also scattered around the room. There was a big TV playing gay porn on mute.

All the men in the posters were white or black with huge cocks, tall and ripped muscled bodies. One, in particular, looked familiar, it was Ms. Deepika that said:

Deepika: Is that you, Frank? From the years you worked as an actor and model! - she pointed to one of the posters, which had a handsome young man on display. Tall, blonde with long hair and green eyes, the sick pack in a good shape, he looked like a surfer. Frank was more mature now, a businessman with short hair and even more muscles than in that picture. But the huge cock and big balls haven't changed a thing! It certainly was Frank "Big Balls" James!
Gemma: Such a happy coincidence! Honey, you should make a curtesy to young Frank there in the poster - she giggles and winks at her pansy husband.
Princess Rekha: eeee no mommy, don't make me do a curtesy to a naked man poster! eeeee pack pack - her protests were in vain, Ms. Gemma uses her hands to get ahold of Princess Rekha's balls from behind, pulling it down, forcing her to do the curtesy.
Deepika: Now why don't you walk around the room and look at each one of the posters like the sissy gay pansy that you are. Mr. Frank will take you for this ride, you just need to ask him. Don't forget you have to call him Sir!
Princess Rekha: eeee pack pack I don't want to look at naked men! I'm not gay eeeeeeiiiii
Gemma: Honey, I thought you wanted to have sex after you begged so much for it - she twirls her hair with her fingers, fluttering her sexy eyelashes.
Princess Rekha: I do, I do pack pack - she answers, thinking about sex and making the chicken noises she makes when making love.
Gemma: So be a good obedient little girl, sweetie, and do as we said - she winks.
Princess Rekha: Please Sir eeeeee take me to the see posters pack pack - she's acting like a shy gay little girl with Ms. Gemma's new boyfriend.

Frank goes with Princess Rekha and they watch each one of the posters together, while the women go behind them.

Gemma: Honey, your sissy clitty is so much smaller than this guy on the poster!
Deepika: Frank's huge cock is bigger though.
Gemma: It really is, I don't even know how I'm still able to walk after what happened - they giggle.
Deepika: Look at this other one, he is so tall, almost as tall as Frank! Princess Rekha, you look like a little girl in front of all of them, you are so short and feminine!
Gemma: Darling, you really are a faggot princess, looking at these hunk naked men.
Princess Rekha: eeee no mommy eee I'm not gay eeeeeiii I promise - she says while whining.
Gemma: So prove to me, honey, by hugging Frank right now. If you are not a faggot sissy, then your sissy clitty won't get hard if you - she uses her hands to force Princess Rekha to hug Frank.
Deepika: Seems like Gemma wasn't the only one happy to meet Frank! - the mistress holds Princess Rekha in place with her hands and forces her to rub her little girl's body all over the tall hot stud.
Gemma: You are doing so good, sweetie. Now time for a kiss - she puts her thick long fingers on Princess Rekha's little girl's mouth and forces her to tongue kiss the alpha male.

The two hot babes are so calm, talking about the gay sex acts like it's a normal occurrence. The pansy has no choice, she's so weak at the sight of the two powerful women, she just obeys like a little girl. She feels Frank's massive tongue penetrating her mouth, his sexy lips are so meaty, they hug and kiss passionately, the women's hands holding and forcing her the whole time so she can't get away, she needs to become a faggot princess for her wife and ex-girlfriend in the pink room.
Now Princess Rekha feels the strong sexy hands of the two goddesses guiding her hands to play with Frank's huge cock and

big balls. She's afraid and starts to cry like a scared Indian bride on her wedding day, overdramatically. It's because Frank's cock is just so big, so beefy, throbbing, and fat, it's nothing like anything she ever touched, including her own cockette.

It's impossible to not compare how Ms. Gemma's new boyfriend is so tall and his cock is humongous and his balls so big and full of man cream that Princess Rekha already tasted. The blonde and the brunette keep talking about it while her strong hands force Princess Rekha's hands to play with Frank's manhood, making the little girl feel so gay.

Gemma: Darling, I know it's the first time you touch a big cock, I know the feeling, I just did the same thing just minutes ago and it changed my life, honey! That's why I'm making you do the same, baby, I want what's best for you.

Deepika: This experience gets even more intense when you touch it with other parts of your body, for example, using your lips - she used her hands to grab Princess Rekha's head and direct her lips all over Frank's body.

Gemma: It's so beautiful to see my little girl worshiping my new hunk boyfriend's tall meaty beefy muscled body! - she also uses her hands to make sure Princess Rekha will kiss every inch of Frank, starting with the lips and then going to the neck, recreating everything she did with him.

Deepika: Tell Mr. Frank how much you love his tall muscled body, Princess Rekha.

Princess Rekha: eeee no, don't make me say gay things, Ms. Deepika pack pack pleeeeease

Deepika: As soon as you put your mouth here, you'll be the gayest faggot princess ever! - she grabs Princess Rekha's hair and suddenly shoves her head on Frank's ass, making her kiss and admire his big balls from behind.

Princess Rekha: eeeee you have big, sexy balls to satisfy my hot goddess wife, Sir, Mr. Frank!

Deepika: Such a good little girl, so obedient. What else? - she guides Princess Rekha's head all over Frank's body. Now she puts it over his long legs.

Princess Rekha: pack pack you are so tall, Mr. Frank, I love being daddy's little girl.
Deepika: Well done! - she uses her hands to force Princess Rekha on Frank's massive cock, she sticks her tongue out of her mouth and licks the precum from the tip.
Princess Rekha: eeee You make love to my goddess hot wifeeeeee the way she deserves, pack pack I love tasting your man creeeeeam in her pussy, Sir aiiiiieeeee
Gemma: You said it so cute, darling! What about my favorite part? - now she's the one forcing Princess Rekha against Frank's big balls, making her suck them and take turns kissing Frank's ass.
Princess Rekha:eeee I love seeing and hearing your big balls bounceeeee and slapping when you make fuck my goddess hot wife! pack pack
Deepika: Do you know that Frank is very supple and can make very creative poses? - she motions to Frank as she uses her sexy hands to lay down the little girl, and Frank squats over Princess Rekha's, putting his legs behind his shoulders, leaving his big balls resting on the pansy's face.
Princess Rekha: eeee my balls are so tiny and minuscule compared to yours, Mr. Frank! pack pack eeee Yours are so heavy, Sir, mine is girly.
Gemma: Sweetie, I wonder if you can take Frank's massive cock in your mouth! Show me, I want to see - Ms. Gemma decided to teach her pansy faggot of a husband to give Mr. Frank a blowjob just like she learned that day. Her flawless hands hold his head and made it bob on Frank's big cock.
Princess Rekha: eeee Your cock is so huge I'm gagging, Mr. Frank, I love feeling your huge balls hitting against my chin pack pack
Deepika: You are a natural faggot cock sucker, Princess Rekha! - she's also helping pansy to suck the hot stud's big dick, inch by inch, the little girl is swallowing everything while the four hands of the two goddesses make her suck cock for the first time.
Princess Rekha: eeeee this is the first time I have a big cock in my body, thank you Mr. Frank pack pack eeeeeee

The little girl was really a natural faggot cock sucker, learning real quickly how to extract every drop of man cream with her gay mouth. She swallowed every drop. It may be the first time she had a big cock in her mouth but it wasn't the first time she ate Frank's man cream. His cock still tasted like Ms. Gemma's pussy and something inside Princess Rekha knew that it was the closest she would ever get from her hot wife's perfect pussy again.

Chapter 27 - First Time

Deepika: That was so hot to watch, however it can get even hotter - she winks at Ms. Gemma and the two hot babes grab Princess Rekha's ears and girly balls with their hands and pull her to the pink little girl's bed.

Gemma: Honey, it will be the first time you'll use your new gay bed! - the blonde goddess twists the little girl's earlobes hard making her cry out loud.

Princess Rekha: eeee pack I want to be in the big bed at the master bedroom, mommy eeeee

Deepika: This is your new place now, Princess Rekha. But don't you worry, Frank is here to lay down with you. Tell daddy you love when he goes to bed with you - her strong hands are squeezing Princess Rekha's pansy balls forcefully.

Princess Rekha: Mr. Frank, I love when you make me your little girl in my new gay beeeeed! - pansy resisted and tried not to cry but she broke into tears by the end of the sentence.

Gemma: Frank, it's Princess Rekha's first time in this bed and I want it to be special. Can you create the most amazing memories in here so every night when she comes to bed my little girl will remember what you did together? - the wife's eyelashes are flustering as she talks with a big smile on her face.

Gemma: I want you to take Princess Rekha's virginity tonight, Frank! Be my little girl's daddy!

Princess Rekha: eeeee nooooooo don't let Mr. Frank take my ass virginity mommy eeeee pleeeeease eeee pack pack eee

The situation was so unbelievable to the faggot princess that she was squawking like a coward chicken. Only a few hours earlier she would never fancy the idea of being turned into a little girl, to become a pansy cuckold, let alone to ever lose her anal virginity! She'd thought it was just a prank but everything else was real, and it made her shake uncontrollably, her little girl's face contorted in a horrified cry and the sounds could be in a Bollywood drama, it was extremely over the top.

While Princess Rekha remains dazed and confused, Mr. Frank knows exactly what to do. The two gorgeous mistresses held Princess Rekha in the bed, on all fours, with her gay face down in a pillow soaked wet with tears. She could feel a female strong hand pulling down her frilly little girl's panties just enough for her faggot ass to be helplessly offered to the hot stud with the huge cock and big balls.

Then Princess Rekha felt pressure in her derriere. Something very big, thick and hard, smooth and warm, was forcing its way inside her pure puckered hole. It was too big and she felt like fainting. Unlike what happened to Mr. Frank and Mr. Gemma lovemaking, when the well-hung man slowly penetrated the woman's tender pussy hole in front of her pansy husband and made her orgasm delightfully, this time he didn't wait until the little girl was ready to accommodate the fat throbbing cock.

In a single stroke, Mr. Frank, the former porn star with the biggest balls ever seen, rammed his huge cock all the way deep inside Princess Rekha rearranging her guts. The white hunk stud deflowered the silly pansy sissy, taking her anal virginity before she could even protest. Princess Rekha felt the most intense feeling in her life, her body and mind conquered by her wife's new white boyfriend, an alpha male making a little girl out of her.

The whole time Ms. Gemma was holding the pansy hands with her perfect strong hands, and Ms. Deepika was using her own hands to hold Princess Rekha in place. The blonde statuesque goddess was whispering in her gay pansy husband's ears:

Gemma: Honey, you are officially a real little girl! Congratulations, you look so gay! - she said lovingly.
Gemma: Now tell daddy how much you love being fucked like a faggot sissy! - she winks at her pansy husband with a broad smile on her face.
Princess Rekha: EEEEEEEEE I love being fucked like a faggot sissy, DADDYYYYeeeeeee pack pack - she squeals like a scared little girl while whimpering.
Gemma: Where's your new place now?
Princess Rekha: My new place is to be daddy's little girl and sleep in the pink room like a faggot princeeeeeeeeeeeess! - pansy was completely broken, trying to enunciate each word but she totally lost in the end because she felt a warm cream filling her insides.

Mr. Frank fucked the gay sissy hard and deep for a long time, her faggot ass became a gape open sore hole and when he exploded his man cream, it overflew. The sexy thick sperm ran down Princess Rekha's legs dripping on the pink bed. The two beautiful women used their hands to flip her over and the solid grip of four sexy strong feminine hands put her head in front of the pool of semen.

Gemma: Darling, tell mommy how hungry you are for daddy's man cream! - the affectionate wife said in a calm soothing voice while twisting her ears.
Princess Rekha: eeeee mommyeeeee I'm a little girl who loveeeees to eeeeat man creeeeam!
Deepika: Dinner time! - she said as they forced the little girl to open her gay mouth and lick the jizz piling up over the bed, slappping her face when the little girl relucted.
Gemma: You are doing it so well, sweetie, here is a little more - the blonde tall woman used her long fingers to scoop the remaining load from Princess Rekha's legs and spoonfed her, making her lick it clean.
Deepika: Princess Rekha is such a good little girl, Gemma! She eats

all the man cream like the faggot sissy that she is!
Gemma: I'm so proud of my little girl, and so is daddy! - she says as she points to Mr. Frank and they all see his huge cock is hard again and ready for action!

Chapter 28 - Special Lullaby

Taking Princess Rekha's virginity was definitely a turn-on to Mr. Frank, the pansy sissy is such an adorable little girl with a perfect gay ass that felt just right. He was hard again in a matter of minutes, it was one of the best sexual intercourse the hot stud ever had, he thought to himself how someone who's believed to be bad in bed only means they are doing it the wrong way. Princess Rekha has huge potential as a faggot gay sissy.

Ms. Gemma also had the best sexual intercourse of her life this very day and noticing how horny the man still is, she wanted to make it up for the lost time so she grabbed his hands and guided him to the master bedroom so they could continue having fun, leaving Ms. Deepika to tuck Princess Rekha in bed.

Gemma: Honey, it's getting late, time for the little girl to sleep - she bats her eyelashes whilst using her hands to tuck her pansy husband in the pink gay bed stained with semen.
Princess Rekha: pack pack I want to sleep in the other bedroom mommy, pleeeease let me sleep with you and daddy eeee pack pack eeiiiii
Deepika: Mommy and daddy will be busy with each other, little girl. I'll be here while they go and have sex, mommy spent too many years without sexual satisfaction due to your tiny sissy clitty, she needs a big cock now! - they giggle and finish tucking Princess Rekha in bed with their sexy hands.
Gemma: Ms. Deepika is right, sweetheart. Good night, my love -

the blonde hotwife kisses Princess Rekha on her lips.

Princess Rekha watches the couple, his loving hotwife and her hunk new boyfriend leaving the room holding hands, they are so tall it makes her feel like a little girl looking at her mommy and daddy. She tries to get up and go after them but Ms. Deepika was there to hold her down with her strong hands, it was impossible to escape.

Ms. Deepika closes the door and stands guard to make sure the little girl won't come after the couple, they will be having sex in the master bedroom, the former love nest of Ms. Gemma and Sanjay, now it's Princess Rekha that dwells in the pink room. She will be able to hear everything, there's even a little hole on the wall where she can watch every steamy act that happens next door.

As soon as they enter the master bedroom, Ms. Gemma and Mr. Frank start to kiss and make out. The naked stud stands so tall, the blonde hotwife needs to be on tiptoes to reach his sexy mouth with her sensual lips to tongue kiss. Her hands wander all over his muscled body, from his broad shoulders and ripped abs, to his big arms and tight butt, the perfect manicured hands finally find her perfect spot: his massive cock and big manly balls.

Gemma: I can't believe how big it is, Frank! - her strong hands manipulating his manhood member, stroking fast and long.
Frank: I love you, Ms. Gemma - he says genuinely between kisses and moans.
Gemma: I think I've fallen out of love with my pansy husband Princess Rekha and now I love you, I want you to live with us and become the man of the house! - they make out vigorously, his hands fondling her big round breasts, her pussy growing wet.
Frank: I want you to have my baby! - his thick tongue now touching her magnificent boobs, feasting on the hard nipples like a hungry baby himself.
Gemma: I always wanted to be a mother, but my faggot pansy of a husband was never able to get me pregnant with his sissy clitty and girly balls. But you Frank, I can tell you are virile with your

huge cock and these big balls contain fertile man cream, perfect to impregnate me - she leads the hunk stud to the bed.

Frank: I'll give you as many babies as you want! - the white man gets on top of Ms. Gemma and opens her legs.

Gemma: Yes, you'll be my little girl's daddy and seed me so I can have your babies! - he licks her pussy, first sucking on her engorged clit and making the hot wife moan so loud it's impossible for Princess Rekha to fall asleep in the pink room.

Frank: I love you, Ms. Gemma - he says between slurps of her thick sweet juices.

Gemma: My faggot pansy of a husband will be the nanny and will raise our babies - she says the words that make her cry in her pillow next room.

Gemma: aaahhh I'll dress her up in a feminine nanny outfit aahhhh, she will look so cute, making curtsies and calling you Sir while rocking the baby hummmm - the moans intensifies, Frank is skillful in his oral skills, sucking and licking the right spots.

Gemma: I'll use my own hands every morning to make sure my little girl looks pristine in her nanny uniform, now that you are the man of the house Princess Rekha doesn't need to work anymore, you are the businessman, the daddy and she is the sissy nanny and maid - the blonde goddess is on the verge of climax so Frank grabs her legs on his shoulders and slides his humongous cock inside of her.

Gemma: My pansy silly gay husband will take your cock too, it feels so good! She's so lucky to be daddy's little girl - Princess Rekha's dicklette is very hard as she hears her hot wife and new white well-hung boyfriend make love so she decides to watch through the peephole.

Gemma: I'll send my little girl to sissy school with Ms. Deepika so she can learn how to be the best faggot princess for us and our babies.

They are both about to cum, they start to kiss and make out as the big cock shaft's throbs and the manly balls pulsate, ready to ejaculate painting Ms. Gemma's pussy walls in white and stuff her womb with white fruitful man cream.

Ms. Deepika explained earlier to Ms. Gemma that scientifically, when a woman orgasm, her cervix opens up allowing the semen to supply the uterus with much-needed seed for her eggs. That's one of the reasons it was difficult for her to get pregnant with a sissy faggot husband like Princess Rekha, not only her sissy clitty was too small to reach further enough to shoot his sissy juices properly, and his girly balls were too small to produce enough fertile pansy cream, but also the lack of orgasm due to the little girl's cries and chicken noises that could never be a turn on.

Frank's alpha male penis, on the other hand, was built to bring women to the peak of pleasure and provide body-shaking orgasms to Ms. Gemma. They came at the same moment and their delightful moans were a lullaby to make Princess Rekha drift into sleep.

Chapter 29 - The Future

Princess Rekha overslept on her first day living as a little girl missing work in the morning, not that she would need to go to work too much, according to Ms. Deepika's ideas that she was about to instill on Ms. Gemma's head. The two hot babes were having breakfast and discussing their impressions about the night before.

Gemma: I'm thrilled with everything that happened, it feels like a dream. At first, I didn't like the things you told me about my pansy husband, although I knew they were true, after all, you dated him and experienced firsthand everything I go through every day - she said while sipping coffee.
Deepika: Yes, I did, and you know Princess Rekha is such a handsome and successful businessman, it makes it even harder when you realize she does have a flaw, a very important one that is hidden. Hidden in a gay closet! - she nods with her head.
Gemma: A tiny little flaw, it is! - she giggles, thinking about her husband's sissy clitty and girly balls.
Deepika: Princess Rekha was like a propellant on my life's journey. I started to understand the importance of tall well hung men in a relationship and grasped how many wives were suffering in silence because they remained loyal to their pansy silly husbands - she said proudly.
Gemma: You help so many couples with your techniques, Deepika!
Deepika: I never wanted to destroy families but to build them,

that's why the sissy husbands are never forgotten, we just add a new member. A big member, if you know what I mean - she winks at the other woman.
Gemma: I wonder what else you have in store for us. I mean, I want to keep my little girl at home as a nanny, she's no longer the man of the house, Frank is.
Deepika: It's something that will happen gradually, in time her company will be in your name and you'll run everything. For now, let's start with baby steps. Her credit card is now rightfully yours. We should go shopping right now!
Gemma: That's a great idea!

     They finished getting ready to go out, Princess Rekha had willfully given her credit card to her hot wife so she could control the finances. The two gorgeous and dominant goddesses drive to the shopping mall and enter a cute store that sells little girls' outfits.

Gemma: I think my little girl will look amazing with this nanny outfit! It's feminine just like her! - she smiles at the dress.
Deepika: Take many pictures every time you buy something for her, so you can tease her when she's working. This is how you keep your little girl on her toes all day while she pretends to be a man! - the brunette lady winks.
Gemma: That's genius!
Deepika: We are also going to buy lots of nice stuff for you and for your new hunk boyfriend, the hot stud with a huge cock and big balls will be pampered with Princess Rekha's hard-earned money - they enter the male department of the store and choose some expensive clothes and accessories for Frank.
Gemma: He certainly will, Frank is now the man in the house and the only man in my life.
Deepika: For now! I know you like white men, they really are superior to Asians like your pansy husband, but you'll have to try different races as well! Black guys are excellent, Latinos are extremely calientes and even Arabians are immensely virile, as long

as they are tall and with big cocks, you'll have fun! - she says as she points to the posters of models in the male underwear department, showing all types of hunk men.
Gemma: You have the craziest ideas, Deepika! And I love them all - her eyes stay longer than they should at the posters, analyzing the content of their boxers, they all carry large packages.
Deepika: When you spoil your new hot boyfriend with the things you buy, you shall take pictures as well and send messages to Princess Rekha at work. Telling her exactly what you are going to do with these things - she grabs her phone and starts to take pictures of the things they are buying.
Gemma: What do you mean?
Deepika: You'll tell her all the fun you are having at home with her new daddy. It will incite her to not work and stay with you, conspiring in favor of the plan of eventually Princess Rekha leaving the company and being a stay-at-home little girl forever!
Gemma: Yes! She will want to be part of the fun, I love my pansy husband so much, it's so cool that he's part of this. You know what Deepika, I'll also buy you a very nice gift because you helped me to save my marriage and soon accomplish the dream of getting pregnant - she picks stuff for Mr. Deepika.
Deepika: Oh thank you, my dear. But you know what, you may not be pregnant now, but you already are a mommy! Your little girl's mommy! - she giggles.
Gemma: You are so right! I want to control every aspect of Princess Rekha's life for her own sake, I want her to look even more effeminate, she has too many muscles! - they stop at the grocery store.
Deepika: We will change your little girl's diet to much more fats and carbs - she grabs ice cream, chocolate, and other fatty food.
Gemma: And what about her constant trips to the gym?
Deepika: They are over! From now on, she will be doing dance lessons and other ladylike activities to become fatter and rounder, all the muscles she cultivated for so long don't suit a sweet gay princess like Princess Rekha!

They leave the mall with many bags in their hands,

naughty ideas for the future in their heads, and wet pussy juices in their panties. It's so much fun to talk about turning pansy husbands into little girls!

Chapter 30 - The Awakening

When she gets home, the house is empty. Sanjay has left to work wearing his suit, Frank is nowhere to be found and Ms. Deepika is busy with her own affairs. Ms. Gemma decides to look at her wedding photo album and reflect on the new chapter of her life.

Ms. Gemma's perfectly manicured hands turn page after page, remembering the reason she married him in the first place and all the good memories of their solid lasting marriage came to her mind at once.

"What am I doing?" - she thought to herself. "I don't want to change anything about Sanjay, I love him just the way he is" - for a moment a small tear popped up in one eye when she recalled how he cried last night. "Sanjay is handsome, smart and so caring. What made me fall in love with him was his way of always making me feel loved and adored, he has this gift called 'the Midas touch', everything he touches turns to gold, he can extract the best of everything, including me. He is a rich and successful businessman because of this" - she wondered.

"Yes, he does have flaws because he is only human and this whole crazy idea that Deepika brought to me... it's my own fault. She's a revengeful ex-girlfriend, he warned me about her when we first met. She used my own idealization of Sanjay as a perfect man to get something innocuous and turned it into a monster" - she came to her senses. "I have to end this for good before this lunatic bad woman ruins my marriage!".

The beautiful blonde wife is a nice person with a pure heart and she fell for Deepika's evil schemes, she was the entrance to only see bad things in her beloved husband and turned a few little trivialities into horrible vicious, and depraved things. But if there was something she learned with Deepika was the fact that she is indeed a powerful woman that is able to do anything she puts her mind to, if she was able to coerce Sanjay to act the way he did without losing him forever, nothing will ever stop her.

So she started her own plan. Texting Deepika and Frank and arranging what was supposed to be a special dinner in a new fancy restaurant that opened inside the club to be paid by Sanjay's credit card. The place was crowded and one could wait months for a reservation, however, Gemma was friends with the owner and arranged a table for that very night! Nobody would skip the chance to have dinner in the most hyped place in town, especially at someone else's expense.

They promptly agreed to go, but little did they know about what was about to happen! She also texted her handsome husband Sanjay and told him to meet her there at the same time and place, but to enter by the back door and go straight to the VIP lounge, which is on the upper floor with a full view of the whole restaurant.

At 7 o'clock, Ms. Gemma was stunning wearing her favorite red saree, in a gesture of embracing her husband's culture. She never believed that Asian men were inferior to white men or any other race, actually, some of the best looking, intelligent, and loving people she knows are Asian! These were all part of Deepika's evil scam to get her husband and her money and she was ashamed she joined such a racist delirium!

The gorgeous blonde woman in the red saree walked at the front door, she was magnificent! Her tall curvy body, long toned legs, and angelic face made everyone turn their heads to see her. She glanced up and could catch Sanjay upstairs, looking at her as well, the only one she ever cared about, which made her smile with her full luscious lips.

Deepika and Frank were at the bar having some drinks, chatting, and waiting for - what they thought - was the perfect prey. A woman with a heart too good to see evil married to one of the most successful, handsome, and rich men in the country. They waved at her and she walked to them. One of the instructions she gave to the mistress and to the former porn actor was that they should be wearing all the gifts she bought for them the day before at the mall, allegedly as a form of humiliating Sanjay to see how Ms. Gemma was willing to spend his money on his nemesis.

What they didn't expect is that, as soon as Ms. Gemma came back to her senses after getting entrance, she used her contacts at the police to charge them for fraud and deception. The hotwife had a special license as a special cop because of the superheroine training and decided to use it to make justice for her adored husband Sanjay.

She reached the bar and told the two scammers they were under arrest, which made them try to run again. She was able to catch them by herself, beat them up, with headlocks and punches, knocking them over. She handcuffed and kicked them from the restaurant and banned them forever from the high society. All the while, Sanjay was watching from above his wife becoming the heroine of the day and bringing justice to his name.

When the cops took the two bandits in the van to prison, she went upstairs to finally meet her husband. She was ashamed but he was understanding and forgave the love of his life. The couple had an amazing dinner and went home.

As soon as they arrived at the house, they went straight to the master bedroom where Sanjay rightfully belongs. While walking down the corridor he could see that the former pink room was back to its normal way.

In bed, Sanjay helped his wife take her saree off and she was wearing the most beautiful pair of lingerie. Small, delicate, and sexy, covering her body just enough to make him want more. She used her caring hands to undress her beloved husband, slowly opening every button of his shirt, taking her time to caress his strong chest.

After undressing the shirt and commenting that he has the strongest muscles and how handsome he is, her affectionate hands went to his pants. Opened it up and unzipped it, caressing his thighs and legs while pulling them down. Then she focused between his legs, still in underwear, rubbing her hands over his cock.

She could see it getting hard and forming a bulge. She slowly took his underwear off and lay down in bed with Sanjay, kissing him entirely from head to toe while telling him how much he means to her.

Gemma: Sanjay, I love you so much! You are such an alpha male, your body turns me on immensely, baby - she kisses his mouth, their tongues dancing with each other as their lips touch.
Gemma: I want to be with you forever, I could never love another man, darling, you are the love of my life - she says as she kisses his neck and down his broad shoulders.
Gemma: I live the happiest life I could ever hope to because you are here with me, I'll always be yours, your loyal wife dedicated exclusively to you, my sweetheart - now she's kissing his ripped abs and feeling their love grow by every second.
Gemma: I want to have sex with you, honey! Right now! - she takes his cock in her mouth, playing with her tongue at the tip, tasting his pre cum, and then she sucks Sanjay's hard cock and plays with his balls using her tender hands.
Gemma: Make me yours, love! - she says as she uses her hands to undress for him, first taking her bra off and showing her magnificent breasts, which Sanjay grabs and sucks on.
Gemma: You make me feel so good, darling, you turn me on so much! - she's moaning as she takes her panties off, it's soaked wet!
Gemma: Make love to me, baby! - the blonde woman got on top of her husband and rode him, thrusting her hips up and down, feeling his cock inside of her perfect pussy.
Gemma: I'll always stay loyal and devoted to you, sweetie, forever! - she says as she feels a tingling sensation in her intimate parts taking over her body.
Gemma: I love you, Sanjay - she says as she cums with her husband's buried inside of her.
Sanjay: I love you, Ms. Gemma - he says back, filling her up with his

semen, not knowing that it was the day they conceived their first child.

And they lived happily ever after.

The end.

Afterword

Congratulations, you have reached the destination of our sexy journey! Now that you are here, I'd like to have some kind of philosophical debate about the fetishes presented in this book and possibly mitigate prejudices and wrong assumptions on the matter.

As mentioned in the Preface, this work was commissioned by a very dear client of mine and although I followed strict guidelines in the matter of content I'm the author, I vouch for freedom of speech and sexuality and in any way discredit myself from the responsibility of touching delicate subjects.

As a sex worker* stigma and persecution is unfortunate inexorable reality. Perhaps because we talk about something extremely complex full of taboos, society tries to shut us down at every corner, after all, sex is dangerous!

For most mainstream religions, the pleasure of sex is a sin. Sex can bring diseases. Sex brings life, which is sacred but also full of responsibilities. Sex can be weaponized against the powerless. Sex exposes our nude bodies and our naked souls, our imperfections, anxieties, the actual fabric of our gender expectations.

Experimenting in first hand the bias in detriment to erotic art, I'll never judge or censor another human being in their sexual expression, as long as we are all consenting adults.

On my personal site, I write monthly articles analyzing popular fetishes, sharing my experiences with each of them. In this book, I've touched subjects I've never written about so I'm going to use this space to talk about them, especially the more delicate ones.

One of the aspects that may be controversial is how the husband's race is used to emasculate him and justify both his transformation into Princess R and how the other man is appealing to Ms. Gemma.

Frantz Fanon in his book "Black Skin, White Masks" talks about how the race subject is profoundly entangled with male sexuality. In the works of this psychiatrist, he points out how the black man is hypersexualized and the Jewish man is hiposexualized, both sides of the same prejudice that see the white race as a standard of perfection, and other races and cultures as less human, they are read as different from what should be the ideal.

As the book's protagonists are an interracial couple living in India, it's impossible to ignore the pervasive Western prejudice of Asian men being sexually inferior to a white man and how it could affect the husband's self-esteem and the sexually inexperienced wife's curiosity.

There are multiple scenes in the story where the husband is coerced to perform things he doesn't want to, from the complete feminization of the character to sexual acts, we watch the husband becoming a puppet in the hands of his wife and ex-girlfriend.

The character is often humiliated because he seems to have feminine traits and his sexuality is mocked. Once again, we use prejudice to play with Humiliation Fetish. There is no man alive that never had his manhood policed and questioned by his peers for showing emotions or acting "feminine".

Sexism and homophobia walk hand in hand causing damage to people as if anything remotely feminine is deemed inferior and could lower a man's value. This is a collective trauma of an entire gender, the fear of being seen as a woman, to be forced to passive homosexual acts to someone who's more of a man. Be it for his physical characteristics (taller, stronger, another race), be it for his personality (manly, aggressive, charming).

In Humiliation Fetish, anything can be used to provoke a sentiment of inferiority, pushing buttons that go deeply into popular imagination and this book touches many of these issues. In my opinion, it's censorship to deny this kind of catharsis to someone who may have suffered and would like to deal with a possible sexual trauma in a roleplay.

I once read an article pointing out how victims of sexual abuse are the main audience of CNC roleplays (consensual nonconsensual), as it allows them to regain control of their sexuality as they are in a safe space under their rules. 80% of women and 40% of men had suffered from sexual abuse at any point of their lives in the US according to the NSVRC, and even those who haven't personally been victims themselves, the numbers are so high that the fear of the possibility can be a trauma in itself.

In tantric massage, a type of genital manipulation with the intention to release repressed sexual energy, it's not uncommon for people to cry as they orgasm, as this kind of intimate physical contact also touches memories and liberates sexual blocks. Erotic roleplays mixed with masturbation can have the same effect on people.

I believe sexual fetishes are a thermometer of our society's ingrained prejudices. As Virginia Woolf shows in her book "A Room of One's One", the father of psychology Sigmond Freud recognized that all his cases of hysteria (how mental illness in women was called in the past) were caused by child sexual abuse, but he decided not to follow through these findings because he didn't want to accuse the family of his respectable and wealthy patients, limiting his work in managing the symptoms.

If we ignore the traumas as Freud did and shut down the conversation on fetishes, not only we won't deal with the problems of people who are alive today, but also it will only expand into something more serious and problematic in everyone's lives.

May us as a society be more gentle to each other, accepting differences. And then these traumas will no longer be reflected in sexuality. Until there, my door will always be open to all you perverts out there. Deep down, we all are.

I'd like to add that, scientifically speaking, there's no sexual or genital difference between males and females of any race or ethnicity. Besides, the vagina's internal size is barely 3 inches, so even if one specific male specimen had a 3 inches long penis, it would be enough for successful sexual intercourse. Most women don't orgasm solely with penetration so the penis size is irrelevant to this purpose. Also, the size and shape of the scrotum (balls) have nothing to do with fertility abilities.

These traits in the story were used solely as tropes, with subsequently redemption at the end when Ms. Gemma realizes she's being manipulated under a trance and comes back to her senses. In no way do we condemn this kind of idea of sexual or social differences between races, cultures, and ethnicities, sexism, homophobic, transphobic, or sexual manipulation and coercive sexual acts, neither with physical violence and domestic abuse.

Erotic art lives in this special realm of sexual fantasy, places where we rarely allow ourselves to go, touching feelings that we keep hidden even from our closest friends and families. A safe space where things don't need to make sense rationally, all that matters is our emotions and the focus is our pleasure.

My mailbox is always open to your opinions and suggestions.

With Love,

Vivian Dash

The Author

Vivian Dash is an online performer of the erotic arts. Specialized in one on one sessions through webcam, phone and text, and custom content such as videos, pictures and stories. Experienced fetishist and open-minded, Ms. Dash takes joy in getting to know people from all over the world and helping them expand their horizons sexually.

Owner of a big butt and an even bigger smile, mutual masturbation is part of her daily routine where she puts to good use her extensive sex toy collection. Her favorite fetishes are Anal (giving and receiving), Jerk Off Instructions (JOI), Squirting (female ejaculation), Femdom and Roleplays.

Her next novel "Eat It!" is a fiction story about a man who's cursed to only be able to cum when he eats his own jizz and looks for a camgirl to help him in this ordeal. Eat It! includes the Fetishes Cum Eating Instruction (CEI) and Jerk Off Instructions (JOI), as well as descriptions of webcam sessions.

Ms. Dash lives with her cat and writes naked, laying down on a hammock at her penthouse's balcony, watching the lights of one of the hottest cities in the world.

Find Vivian Dash on her website www.viviandash.com

Vivian Dash

Printed in France by Amazon
Brétigny-sur-Orge, FR